CROW MUSIC

A Novel

(Book 5 of the Gumbeaux Sistahs series)

JAX FREY

Tales of the Friendship Bench

Printed in the United States of America
First Printing 2022

ISBN paperback:

Cover Illustration: Crow Music by Jax Frey

This book is dedicated to Betty Bruce,
a fighter, a friend, and a sistah to the end.

Native American beliefs: Crows are seen as a symbol of transformation, change, and intuition. They are believed to communicate with the spirit world and act as spiritual guides.

When you see or hear a crow, God is calling.

ON ENLIGHTENMENT

"You are here for no other purpose than to realize your inner divinity and manifest your inner enlightenment. Foster peace in your own life and then apply the Art to all that you encounter."

—**Morihei Ueshiba**

"Your own Self-Realization is the greatest service you can render the world."

—**Ramana Maharshi**

"…the past gives you an identity and the future holds the promise of salvation, of fulfillment in whatever form. Both are illusions."

—**Eckhart Tolle**

"You are never alone. You are eternally connected with everyone."

—**Amit Ray**

"According to Vedanta, there are only two symptoms of enlightenment, just two indications that a transformation is taking place within you toward a higher consciousness. The first symptom is that you stop worrying. Things don't bother you anymore. You become light-hearted and full of joy. The second symptom is that you encounter more and more meaningful coincidences in your life, more and more synchronicities. And this accelerates to the point where you actually experience the miraculous."

—**Deepak Chopra**

"There is a candle in your heart, ready to be kindled.
There is a void in your soul, ready to be filled.
You feel it, don't you?"

—Rumi

"Let me tell you why you're here. You're here because you know something. What you know you can't explain, but you feel it. You've felt it your entire life, that there's something wrong with the world. You don't know what it is, but it's there, like a splinter in your mind, driving you mad. It is this feeling that has brought you to me. Do you know what I'm talking about?"

—Morpheus from *The Matrix*

BECAUSE I'M SIXTY
BY JAX FREY

I've said it for years, and today I'll say it again:
Sixty is my cut-off age.

That's when all the BS stops. That's the age when I'll stop being afraid to really live. By sixty, I'll already have lived a long life, so I might as well do what I love. I'll stop holding back my public opinions out of fear that they may affect my business. I will stop dieting and start eating whatever the hell I want. Take note, I mostly want to eat food that is healthy, but after sixty, when the mood strikes, cookies for breakfast will be forever off the forbidden list.

And at sixty, I'll let all my secrets out. Like the fact:

- That I'm psychic, still sexy, and a tad bit psycho.
- That I'd rather read and paint than attend any small-talk party.
- That I think my crow's feet are cute.
- That I've moved over thirty times in my life because I like living in new places rather than just visiting them.
- That I hug and even kiss trees and love lying in piles of freshly fallen leaves.
- That I create paintings and write books that are important to me, and I love it when they become important to others as well.
- That new experiences are healing and necessary for my expansion.

- That I admire authenticity in all its fascinating forms.
- That I love the creative life I've designed for myself.
- That using my chainsaw makes me feel like a badass.
- That I need 80% alone time and 20% dance time.
- That I still have feelings for a long-ago love.
- That dogs are perfect beings. (Especially my pugs, Lucy and Ethel.)
- That a good martini or red wine can still occasionally surprise me with their luxuriousness.
- That using the f—k word in a sentence sometimes works better than an exclamation point.
- That I dream of RV-ing across country with a group of strong, funny women in vintage trailers.
- That social snubs can no longer touch me. Snub away!
- That I believe that religions are all right—and all wrong.
- That spending time with my children is the best time of all.
- That to me a coffee house is better than a bar—most of the time.
- That I love dressing like a fashion plate and a paint-spattered hobo—equally.
- That energy spots exist on the earth, and I try to seek them out when I can.
- That pain scares the shit out of me, but being dead doesn't.
- That my girlfriends make everything better.
- That I feel to my core that we are all one and part of a Greater One. Period.
- That I know we never die, so I don't sweat it.
- That God means more to me than anything.
- That I can look at people with more love in my heart now than ever before.

Because I'm sixty. And it's a good place to be.

LIST OF MAIN CHARACTERS

Dawn Berard—co-owner of The Gumbeaux Sistahs Gallery and owner of family business Berard Accounting. Was married to Dan Berard, now widowed.

Lola Broussard—Landscaper, lawyer, activist, best friends with Dawn and married twice to same man, Bud Broussard.

Judith Lafferty—artist and co-owner along with Dawn Berard of The Gumbeaux Sistahs Gallery.

Bea Walker—retired, widow, unofficial leader of the Gumbeaux Sistahs, lay minister with an Episcopal Church.

Helen Hoffmann—owner of Body Workings Essential Oils Company, Reiki and massage therapist, widow.

Lynn Lamoree—Tarot reader, old friend of Dan Berard's.

Sondraya—Astrology, Palm, and Tarot Reader. Lives in Sedona.

CHAPTER 1

Dawn Berard knelt in her new vegetable garden behind her house, pulling weeds and cussing loudly. The radishes were plentiful, and the tomatoes were going gangbusters, so she wasn't cussing the state of her vegetables. It was a warm summer morning, the kind of day that makes you think of sunflowers, so she wasn't cussing about the weather. She knelt on a soft rubber gardener's cushion, so she wasn't cussing about any physical discomfort. She wasn't even cussing her troublemaking best friend, Lola Broussard, a professional landscaper who had talked Dawn into putting in the garden in the first place. Truth be told, Dawn would almost always rather sit on her deck with an iced tea and buy all her veggies from the farmers market. But when she was in the mood, she didn't mind caring for the garden. It made her feel more connected with the earth and her southern roots which included generations of Cajun women with garden patches. She would never admit that to Lola, who would just say "I told you so," and get much too much pleasure from saying it too.

But Dawn wasn't in the mood for gardening, or anything else, and had not been in the mood for a while. Somehow, slowly over the last few months, an anxiety had crept into her composition. It was hard for her to describe, but the best she could do was say that it felt as if a murky puddle of sludge-like depression had crept into her house, covered her shoes, and was lapping at her ankles. It was difficult to get out of bed in the morning lately because she knew she would be stepping away from the relief of dreams and stepping back into brain fog and murkiness.

She tried writing a poem about the feeling one night with a rather large glass of wine at her side.

Night

Quiet neighbor noises
Car doors, goodbyes, fading smiles
Empty the wine glass as
Somewhere in the dark a hound cries out to the moon
Turn off the TV
A vacuous hum in her ears
The cat wants in and
She wants out.
Switch to coffee and
Huddle against the back
Of the big, blue chair
That once belonged to him
It smells like leather and cold
The only one left in the house
In love with her
Is herself
And that too was questionable.

Ever since Dan, her husband of over thirty years, had passed of a heart attack, things that used to excite her didn't seem important anymore. The Gumbeaux Sistahs gallery that she owned with her business partner, Judith Lafferty, was doing such a bang-up business, they had even hired a gallery manager to run the place. It freed up Judith's time to create art for the gallery and Dawn's time to do—whatever. Dawn still visited the gallery, but it was mostly to meet her four best friends who called themselves the Gumbeaux Sistahs, Lola, Judith, Bea, and Helen, for coffee. The gallery had a coffee and baked goods section with tables and chairs, making it a favorite meeting place for the women as well as many in the community.

Lately, the murkiness Dawn felt was getting worse. She had seen a therapist a few times about her growing listlessness. Dr. Wagner recommended that she try something new, such as volunteering, to bring some zest back into her life. So Dawn started working at the Habitat for Humanity in their Women Build program. It consisted of a group of women who helped a low-income person or family in the community to actually build their own home. She showed up for a few hours on Saturdays and swung a hammer where the building supervisor told her to while other women worked around her. It was a wonderful cause, and she found it rewarding because she could get out of her head once a week and was genuinely helping someone. But Dawn could tell it was not solving her problem. The murkiness grew. She feared it would encompass her entire being, and she occasionally had to fight back panic attacks at the thought.

On top of this, weird things had been happening to her. She hadn't told anyone about it because she didn't want them hauling her off to the looney bin. She actually tried to ignore it because it just did not seem real. She thought she might be having hallucinations. But today, she had to acknowledge it. The fact was—crows were following her.

It happened again that morning. A black feather had floated down from the sky and landed on her shoulder as she knelt in the garden. She lifted it and brought it to her face to examine its black luminescence, then she looked up to see six or seven crows in the branches of the tree above. They all seemed to be staring at her. And that wasn't all—not by a long shot. In the last week, she'd had other black feathers show up without warning. One almost landed in her coffee as she sat on her deck two days ago. Another sat on her door mat as she left the house to go shopping. Another had even floated through her half closed car window, just before she finished rolling it up. There was even a confused crow who obviously thought it was a rooster because it woke her up every morning, cawing at her bedroom window. And she would never forget the crow who only just missed pooping on her as she stood on the sidewalk. It sat above her on the power lines running from the roof of her house to her garage. Talk about getting her attention!

She kept asking herself, *"Is this real?"*

Dawn found it all pretty annoying but also puzzling. Was she crazy? Or maybe it was crow mating or molting season? Crow mating, molting, or being freaky season—it had to one of them.

But this time, she stood up in her garden holding the sleek purple-black feather and shouted to the trees, "No one can tell me I'm crazy. This is real!" The crows continued staring.

She still did not know what to make of it, and it sure didn't improve her mood any.

Today she was in an extra dark mood, and it wasn't just the crows, although they were bad enough. No, it was all about the letter that arrived in the mail that morning. She pulled the envelope out of her apron pocket and stared at it for the tenth time.

The return address was a New Orleans location, and the sender's name was Lynn Lamoree. Dawn thought it was such a pretty name. Too bad she had to curse its existence because the letter was addressed to Dan, Dawn's husband, who had passed two years ago. The letter read:

Dear Dan:

> *Hope this letter reaches you. I don't have your email, so I had to resort to snail mail. Just thought I'd let you know that I'll be revisiting the stomping grounds from our trip together, thirty years ago this month. Can you believe that it's been that long? It was such a*

profound journey. Thinking of you with fond memories. Email me!

Love,
Lynn
Fast-Lynn@gmail.com

Dawn stared at the letter and her hands shook. She felt tears spring to her eyes, as they had been doing all morning since the mail arrived. Her stomach felt nauseous, so she pushed herself off her knees and sat on the weeding cushion in the shade and let grief run its course. Except it wasn't just the usual grief this time. It was grief mixed with betrayal.

The letter said there was a trip her husband had taken with this Lynn person thirty years ago. With renewed horror Dawn thought of how she and Dan had just celebrated their thirty fifth wedding anniversary right before he died. As if it were written on a glaring marquis in her brain, the words *Dan took a trip with that woman WHILE WE WERE MARRIED!* There was no other way to spin it—this was a fact.

Dawn reached into her apron pocket again and this time pulled out her phone. She texted a group message to her Gumbeaux Sistahs that said simply, "Emergency meeting. GS gallery. 9AM tomorrow!"

She shoved her phone back into her pocket, looked around for crows, and muttered, *"Love, Lynn—my ass!"*

CHAPTER 2

At nine AM the next morning, five women met at the Gumbeaux Sistahs gallery on Columbia Street in Covington, Louisiana. The gallery was named after the five long-time, close friends and was owned by Dawn and Judith Lafferty, a local artist. The gallery featured many pieces painted by Judith and other local artists' work as well. One corner of the gallery held a coffee counter and pasty case, and that was where the Sistahs huddled this morning.

The group called themselves the Gumbeaux Sistahs because they'd become such close friends that they felt like sisters, and because they all loved to cook and eat excellent gumbo. They were extremely competitive about who cooked up the best gumbo and to date, not one of them agreed with the other on a winner since they were all convinced that they themselves should wear the crown.

Since they'd formed their little group years ago, several other Gumbeaux Sistahs groups had formed with the Sistahs' help. On occasion, the groups got together for a big cook-off of, of course, gumbo.

But this morning, the Sistahs were sticking to coffee and Helen's scones. Helen was a body worker who famously concocted custom essential oils for her generously paying clients. By agreement, she also kept the pastry case filled with her scones. They found out the hard way what happened if the case ran out of scones for customers who craved her confections. One woman came in with gleeful anticipation of a scone and walked out dismayed by the empty pastry case, only to take matters in her own hands. Covington is a small place where everyone knows where everyone else lives, so this didn't prove difficult.

She showed up at Helen's house, where Helen lived with her adopted son, Cooper. The woman suggested that Helen get busy with scone-baking in her kitchen right then and there. Since that day, Helen was not anxious to repeat the pushy-scone-woman experience, and there had never been another lack in the pastry department.

Helen offered Dawn a scone and then held the platter out to the other Sistahs, Bea Walker, Lola Broussard, and Judith Lafferty. The Sistahs had never been known to turn down a bowl of gumbo, a glass of wine, or one of Helen's scones.

Judith had her two pugs, Lucy and Ethel, with her today, as she often did. They sat quietly surrounding her soft colorful long skirt and waited for their share of a scone, which would inevitably come. Judith's many bracelets clinked as she handed bits of confection to her beloved furry friends. Judith was the newest member of the Sistahs, having been recruited just a few years ago. If truth be known, it had been a mandatory recruitment. The Sistahs could be forceful, and every time Judith thinks about her unorthodox induction, which involved a gentle kidnapping of sorts, she does the exact same thing— she shakes her head, laughs softly, and feels an overwhelming swell of gratitude. The Sistahs were one of the best things to happen in her previously lonely life as an introverted artist. Since that time, she and Dawn had opened the gallery together and enjoyed success with it in every sense.

Bea reached across the pastry counter for the plate of scones which turned out to be quite a reach for her tiny self. A widow of many years and a retired customer service trainer, Bea was known as the Velvet Hammer in the group. They called her this because she was the unofficial leader of the group due to her tendency to "mother" every person on earth. If there was a hurricane in the Gulf of Mexico or a sick acquaintance in the hospital, you could count on Bea's somewhat pushy reminders of how to handle the situation or what needed to be done. There were times when one of the Sistahs or other felt Bea was being too pushy. After all, they were all grown-ass women. They might be tempted to tell Bea that they'd already had one mother, and that one was plenty enough. But they always gave her a pass because they knew she had a heart of gold and that she really cared for them. They conceded that her intentions were good and, besides, Bea was usually right about everything and gave good advice. Also, they loved their friend dearly with her twinkly, humor-loving eyes and forever-present little straw hat which half-covered her greying head of hair.

Last to get her scone was the sistah with the biggest mouth, or one that at least matched Dawn's in volume. Lola Broussard was Dawn's best friend of many years. She was the only married sistah in the group, having married Bud Broussard twice with an unfortunate break in between weddings. And as she often reminded him, "And twice is enough, Bud, so mind yourself!" She and Bud shared a love of landscaping, and both came from nursery business backgrounds. Lola was a landscape architect, but also had a side degree in law. She liked to say that since the Sistahs tended to get themselves in so much trouble, often legal trouble, that it really came in handy. Bud owned the Broussard Nursery in New Orleans, and they lived together in Covington. Lola, dressed in her usual denim overalls for work, was never one to hide her opinions, and she had the fiery red hair and freckles to prove it. She spoke up loudly, "Alright, Dawn, I've got my scone and my coffee, and I can act like a human being now. So tell us, what's with the emergency meeting?"

Dawn was not her usual humor-loving self this morning, and the Sistahs noticed it immediately. She had been up most of the night thinking of the letter from Lynn Lamoree, and when she finally slept, she dreamed of crows sitting on the end of her bed cawing their brains out. She was usually outfitted in the most expensive clothes of the group with never a hair out of place in her brown bob. But today she had on old jeans, sloppy, worn loafers, and a wrinkled white shirt that she'd obviously just thrown on. She opened her mouth and said, "Sistahs, I hardly know where to begin."

Bea, sensing her distress, said softly, "Just spill it, dear. You know we're all here for you."

Dawn dug into her purse and plopped several items down on the table in front of the group. "This will help explain."

The Sistahs looked over the items. There were three black feathers and a worn looking envelope. Lola said sarcastically, "Are we supposed to guess? OK, I'll go first. This must a letter from some birds to remind you to not be so stingy at the bird feeder."

Helen chuckled, "Lola, you sound just like Dawn."

"I know, we've been friends way too long," said Lola with a grin.

"Wait, I know," Helen said, laughing, "It's a letter delivered by birds—so it's air mail! No wait, maybe the letter was delivered by carrier pigeon! Do they have black carrier pigeons?"

"Better carrier pigeons than a stork!" said Lola, getting into it now.

With a slight smile, Bea took one look at Dawn's disgusted expression and said, "That's probably enough kidding around, dears. Dawn, I can see you're upset. What's going on?"

Dawn sighed and began. "OK, you're not going to believe all this anyway, but here goes. There's actually two parts to this, and I'm not sure which is more disturbing. The first part has to do with the feathers. They're from crows. Suddenly crows are everywhere! They wake me up in the morning, they swoop by me in the garden, they call to me all day from the big oak tree in the yard, they drop feathers on me, and, get this, one of them even tried to poop on me!"

"You're kidding," said Lola, taken aback. "That's actually a little creepy. Gives me Hitchcock vibes. Wait, do you need for me to take you to the doctor or are you already on medication?"

"Oh hush, Lola. I really need help here!" said Dawn.

"Do you think it means something, dear?" asked Bea, seriously.

"That's exactly what I don't know. Does it? I thought Helen might know seeing as how she's so woo woo and all," explained Dawn.

Helen looked at her friend thoughtfully and said slowly "Actually, I do know something about this, but I'm not sure you're going to go like it."

This got the Sistah's attention. Lola whispered woefully, "Oh boy. Here comes trouble."

Helen went on, "Dawn, I've studied signs from nature, and I know a bit about totem animals. Turns out that the crows are symbols of introspection and rebirth. They are the messengers of God. Are they cawing at you a lot?"

"Oh my God, yes," said Dawn, rolling her eyes. "All freaking day."

"Then they are either telling you that the universe is taking care of you—or that your spirituality needs looking after. One message will produce peace in your heart, and the other will cause anxiety. Have you been anxious lately?"

To the Sistahs' surprise, tears spring into Dawn's eyes. She stood up abruptly and turned away from them, hiding her face.

"Oh dear," said Bea, reaching out for her friend to place a comforting hand on her shoulder.

Lola looked shocked. "Dawn, what's going on? I've never seen you like this before."

"Sorry we teased you before, Dawn. This looks serious," said Judith.

"Aw jeez, sistahs. I'm sorry I'm such a sap. It's all just too much right now."

"I never knew that birds could make you cry. I'll have to watch out for that…" said Lola, trying to tease a smile from her friend.

"Birds can make you cry," retorted Dawn hotly, pointing at Lola. "And bird-brains too!" But a smile almost broke through on her face.

"Come sit back down and tell us everything, dear," encouraged Bea.

Dawn fell back into her chair and took a sip of her coffee, resetting her nerves. "Look, y'all. I haven't said anything for the last few months, but I've been kind of losing it. I don't even know what's wrong. I feel anxious, yes, and nervous, and bored silly, and flat-out depressed. And I think it's more than just grief over Dan. I guess it feels like something's missing. I mean, I can't believe I'm complaining here, which is why I haven't said anything before this. I mean, my accounting firm is being run by my kids, and they're doing a great job. And our gallery is kicking butt, so no complaints there. And I have wonderful friends, thank God! What would I do without you, Bea, Helen, Judith?" She hesitated for moment, hiding a smile, because she knew what was coming.

"Hey, you left me out! What am I? Chopped liver?" demanded Lola with a huff, which made Dawn laugh out loud.

Bea redirected their teasing, as usual, and brought them back on track. "So what do you think it is, Dawn?"

"I wish I knew. But it has something to do with those damn crows. If I knew for sure, I would do something about it."

"Are you sure about that?" asked Helen, pointedly.

"What do you mean?" asked Dawn.

"Nothing personal. It's just that sometimes it's hard to make changes. It's sometimes hard to even see the changes that need to be made."

Judith added, "Boy, that's true. We've all been through those moments in life where it's time to head in a different direction to make a much-needed change. But sometimes, we find ourselves kicking and screaming because change can be hard. Remember when I lost my job at the art museum? All I wanted to do is fight tooth and nail with those responsible. But the loss of that job brought me to be friends with y'all, and to open this gallery. Some changes are hard to start, but they led to some wonderful things."

"So what do you think needs to change, Dawn?" asked Bea, quietly, watching her friend closely.

Dawn scrunched up her face miserably. "I wish I knew."

"Well, if I know one thing, it's that anyone who has crows chasing them up the street has something going on in their life, and they'd better pay attention," said Lola, pointing to her friend. She added seriously, "It sounds like anxiety, and it sure doesn't sound like fun, sistah."

"I'm trying to pay attention, I really am. But pay attention to what?" asked Dawn, getting frustrated.

Helen hesitated. "I think I know, Dawn. In a case like this, it's sometimes about spirituality—however that form takes for you."

Dawn was surprised and protested, "But I go to church. Y'all know I do. And I do pray. I'm not sure how to get more spiritual unless I check into a nunnery or something."

"Could it be that God wants you to be closer right now?" asked Helen thoughtfully.

"But how do I do that? Is there an ashram in Tibet in my future?" Dawn with an uneasy laugh.

"I can't say," said Helen with a shrug. "But now that you know this, you can pay better attention to what the universe is trying to show you."

"It does feel important, doesn't it, dear?" asked Bea. "I think that Helen may be right."

"I think you should just give it a little time and maybe pray about it," continued Helen.

"I'll try anything," agreed Dawn. "I'm so tired of being anxious and depressed and truly exhausted all the time. The universe is wearing me out."

"I'll say," teased Lola. "You're a mess, sistah."

Bea added, "I think keeping a watchful eye on the universe, following up on things that present themselves to you, and being patient is your best course of action. Something will come to you."

"That sounds right to me." Dawn looked thoughtful for a moment. "And I have something else I need to tell you. I can't tell you how upset I am about it. As if I didn't have enough going on."

"Just spill it, Dawn. You've been doing fine so far," Bea said.

"You know, now that I think of it, maybe it's the universe messing with me even more. Maybe it's all part of the same changes that are being asked of me."

"OK, you're killing me, Dawn. Out with it," said Lola, smacking the table top.

Without saying anything, Dawn reached over and picked her rumpled envelope up off the table. She plunked it down on the table in front of Lola and then simply said, "OK, read this and tell me what you make of it. It came by mail yesterday."

Lola reached for the envelope. As she pulled out the letter, a business card fell out and landed on the table. Helen pick it up and read it out loud:

Lynn Lamoree
Healer, Psychic, Tarot Reader

The card gave a New Orleans address, phone number, and email.

"Oh my, now this looks interesting," said Helen. "What does the letter say, Lola?"

Lola read the one page letter out loud. As she read her eyes grew wide and she finished with silence, staring at Dawn. "What the actual hell is this, Dawn?"

All of the Sistahs looks shocked except Dawn who shook her head and said, "I wish I knew."

Lola broke in, "This Lynn person must not know that Dan has passed. That much is apparent. But wait just a minute here. This says that their trip together was thirty years ago. But I know for a fact that Dan and you would be married for thirty-six years in August. But that means . . ." Her face looked stricken.

"Oh no," groaned Judith. Bea and Helen exchanged worried glances.

"Look," said Dawn, "I know what it means, alright. It means that about thirty years ago my husband took his married ass on a trip with this Lynn Lamoree!"

"Did you know about this?" asked Helen in a whisper.

"No, I did not," said Dawn miserably. "I've been wracking my brains to think what was going on in our lives at that time—where we were living then and all that, and I think I know." She sighed deeply and continued. "I don't like to think about this—ever. But there was a short period of time in the early years of our marriage that Dan and I hit a rough patch. It was right when we were starting the business, and it was tough going for a while. The business was new, and we were growing it as fast as we could, but there were many months when we didn't know if we would make it. In fact, Dan took a temporary accounting job at an oil company in Covington. It was so stressful. He was working two jobs, and the kids were little. There was one argument after another. Neither one of us was very happy."

"I didn't know about that," said Lola.

"Yeah, well, I'd like to forget about it myself," said Dawn with a grimace. "Especially since Dan actually moved out for about two months. It was a pretty brutal time for us."

Lola gasped and Bea spoke up, "So you think this trip happened during the time when you lived apart?"

"I don't see when else it could have happened."

"I'll be damned," swore Lola. "I'm sorry, Dawn, but I just want to kill Dan."

"Too late for that." Dawn's voice was sarcastic, but deep with sadness. "I can't believe he never told me."

"What are you going to do?" asked Judith.

"What can she do?" asked Bea, shaking her head.

Lola stood up, shaking with anger. "Well personally, I would just kill to know about that damn trip and this woman Lynn Lamoree, wouldn't you, Dawn?"

Dawn sighed, "I don't think I have any choice, Lola. I have to find out."

"Atta girl!" shouted Lola.

"But how?" asked Judith.

Helen held out the business card that she'd kept in her hand since Lola opened the letter. "Her card says she's a healer, a psychic, and a tarot reader. That's pretty interesting."

"Yeah, yeah," said Dawn, reaching for the card and staring at it. "She's probably interesting, and smart, and gorgeous too. Oh God! I really am going to have to kill her, aren't I?"

"I'll help you," nodded Lola, loyally.

Helen giggled, "Oh dear, I sure hope you two are kidding, but I wouldn't bet on it."

Judith smiled, "I'd say there was a fifty/fifty chance on that."

"Let's all calm down, dears," said Bea. "No one is killing anyone. We need to think about this."

"Shoot, you're a killjoy, Bea," said Lola. She winked at Dawn.

"Look," said Bea, reasonably, "If you want to find out about this woman, you need to go about it in a straightforward manner."

"Bea is right," agreed Helen. "You just need to contact her and be honest about who you are and what you want to know about her and Dan."

"Or..." said Lola slowly, with a glint in her eye, "You can make an appointment for a tarot reading with her and then find out about her, posing little questions that lead to a conversation about spiritual journeys and Dan. You know, take the sneaky route."

"I think being honest is a much better idea," said Helen, looking to Bea for back up.

Judith cut in, "But you know, Lola may have something there. This woman might actually be more inclined to tell you things if she doesn't know who you are."

"That's true," said Lola, triumphantly.

"Honesty is always the best policy," insisted Bea.

Dawn looked from one sistah to another, then made a decision and slapped the letter down on the table. "Sistahs, I need to know about this woman. So the sneaky route it is!"

Lola clapped, and Bea groaned. "Are you sure, dear?"

"Bea, I know that you mean well, and that this is not going to be a fun task. It's going to be painful. But at least doing it under cover will make it more of an adventure. And, like Judith said, she may be more inclined to open up to me if she doesn't know I'm Dan's wife."

"That's right," said Lola, jumping to her feet. "C'mon Dawn. Let's go to your place and start lying our asses off!"

CHAPTER 3

Dawn and Lola sat in Dawn's home office with ice clinking in glasses of sweet tea. They both leaned over the computer as Dawn's fingers rested on the keyboard.

"Dawn, what we're doing feels about fifty percent right and a hundred percent wicked, don't you think?" asked Lola.

"I don't really care right now, Lola. Do you?"

"Not at all," answered her best friend and worst influence. "Read me what we have so far in that email."

"OK, here goes. It says:

Dear Lynn:

I got your letter and it was so good to hear from you. Hope all is well on your end. Everything is as good as can be expected here in Covington. I was so happy to hear that you are taking that amazing journey once again. And I'll ask you a special favor: as you go on this trip, shoot me an email and remind of where we went. I'll relive the adventure vicariously. I can't wait to hear all about it.

Sincerely,
Dan

There. What do you think?" asked Dawn.

"Pretty good for a dead guy," answered Lola.

Dawn's mouth dropped, and she asked furiously, "What's wrong with you, Lola? That's my deceased husband you're talking about!" But Dawn couldn't help but laugh at her outrageous friend.

Lola pointed at Dawn's face and said, "There it is! There's that smile." Lola looked up and said loudly, "Sorry Dan. I only said it to make Dawn laugh."

"Dan would have been falling over laughing," said Dawn sadly. "He always thought you were funny. Demented, but funny."

"Yeah, I liked him too," said Lola, putting her hand on Dawn's shoulder. "All the more reason why I want to find out who this Lynn chick is. Am I right?"

"You are. And I think the email sounds pretty good. It's a little bit vague because we don't know how long Dan was with her or the details of their relationship. Did all this happen just during that period of time when we were separated, or was it something more?"

"Agreed," said Lola. "Ready for blast off?"

Dawn looked from her friend to the keyboard, and before she could change her mind, her hand bolted out and hit "Send."

"Well, I guess we're committed now," said Lola, wiggling her eyebrows at her friend. "Now, on to the second part of our diabolical plot." She picked up Dawn's phone and handed it to her.

"Oh my gravy," said Dawn, anxiously. "Maybe I should rethink this."

"I think you've overthought it enough already," said Lola, exasperated. "How else do you propose to know this woman?" She put her hands on her hips, "Look if you're afraid, give me that phone and I'll do it."

"Oh no," said Dawn, turning her back on her friend. "You'll just say something crazy and scare her off."

"You're probably right, so that settles it. You have to do it. So, go ahead."

Dawn closed her eyes for a moment breathing deeply. Then she opened them and looked at her phone in horror like it was covered in slime. She really did not want to make this call. But then thoughts of Dan crowded in. She thought of their many years together and tried to push away the doubt that their happiness had been forced. That it had worked around a relationship he'd had with Lynn. It was possibly even an affair. She knew she had no choice. "Alright, dammit. Here goes."

She dialed the number on the business card in her hand. The line connected and a strong, feminine voice answered, "Hello, this is Lynn."

"Uh, hello Lynn. This is Dawn Boudreaux," she said, using her maiden name. "Someone gave me your business card, and I thought I would call and make an appointment with you for a reading."

"OK, nice to meet you, Dawn," said Lynn. She hesitated for a moment then went on. "When did you want to come in? It will have to be late next week. I'm afraid I'm in California right now on a spiritual trip of sorts."

"I'll bet the weather there is a lot nicer than ours right now," said Dawn, nervously, peaking out the window to her garden which was soaking from a sudden afternoon rainfall.

Lynn chuckled. "You're certainly right about that. Santa Barbara is glorious right now. I can't wait to go outside every day."

"That's hard to imagine," said Dawn, pacing the room. Lola waved her hands, signaling "*What did she say?*" Dawn ignored her.

"So, how's Thursday at eleven work for you? I'll be back by then."

Dawn thought for quick second then said, "That's good for me. Can you text me your address?"

"Will do," said Lynn. "And meanwhile, you text me your city of birth, your time of birth, and you birthdate. I'll need them for your astrology reading. See you Thursday, Dawn."

"Thanks. And have a great trip." Dawn hung up the phone, cringing, and looked at Lola.

"How did she sound?" asked Lola.

"Really nice," said Dawn scowling. "Dammit."

CHAPTER 4

Dawn sent the following email to Lola the next morning:

"Lola, you asked me to keep you posted about this, so here goes. Lynn actually emailed Dan back last night! Here's what she wrote:

Dear Dan:

> *You'll never guess where I am.*
> *I'm sitting on the porch of my yurt at the White Lotus Foundation in Santa Barbara, CA. Remember this place? It's still beautiful, secluded, and sooooo quiet. We had such a fantastic time here, didn't we?*
> *Getting ready for yoga class, but I'm grateful to relive the memories with you in this moment.*
> *You need to come to this place again. You had one of your first break-throughs right in this very spot!*

Love,
Lynn

"I'm dying over here, Lola. Can you believe her? Does she know that Dan has a wife? Did she know back then? I can't help but wonder if Dan was still alive, would he drop everything and go meet her out in California. She makes it sound so inviting, doesn't she? Shoot it makes me want to go too. Talk later—Dawn."

She closed her laptop and sat thinking about the crows, and Lynn, and how events in her life seemed about to explode. She felt that forces were coming together for a purpose, and in her heart, she felt it had something to do with things that had happened to her as a child. Things she'd never told anyone about. Not even Lola. Dawn had a secret.

CHAPTER 5

Lynn Lamoree

The following Thursday, Dawn walked up the front sidewalk to the old two-story pink house in the Carrollton section of New Orleans. The morning sun fell on the native plants in the front yard. She recognized blue phlox, elderberry, Louisiana iris, and coral honeysuckle, among others. As she drew closer to the house, she heard tinkling bells and a low-timbre wind chime. Tiny flashes of light greeted her eyes from miniature mirrors strung throughout the garden, suggesting fairy activity. The house was welcoming with warmth, and Dawn wished she could just sit for a moment by herself on the wooden bench tucked in a corner of the front porch.

As she raised her hand to ring the doorbell, a crow cawed at her from a nearby tree. Dawn called out to the bird, "I don't freakin' believe it! You followed me here?"

Then before she could press the doorbell button, the door swung open.

"And there she is," thought Dawn, staring at the woman on the other side of the stoop, but keeping her face neutral. She still did not know if this woman was friend or foe.

"Dawn Boudreaux," said the woman, not asking, but stating a fact.

"Yes I am. Lynn?"

"I sure am," answered the woman with a broad, warm smile. She was shorter and rounder than Dawn with long, white hair. Her intelligent, ice-blue eyes looked deeply into Dawn's as she held out a hand and took hold of Dawn's. Dawn felt as if some sort of information was exchanged with just that touch.

"Come on in," Lynn said and stood back, making room for Dawn to pass. Lynn wore a cream peasant blouse and a long matching cream cotton skirt. Several dozen bracelets were divided between her two wrists, and crystals dangled from her necklaces and her earrings. Baby-blue toe nail polish peeked out from her bare feet. Her smile was warm and wise.

"It's good to meet you, Dawn." Lynn suddenly gathered Dawn into her big arms for a crushing warm hug.

Dawn submitted to the hugging as her eyes took it all in—from Lynn's bohemian vibe to the bright purple walls of her living room. She followed Lynn into a back sunroom with a round table in the center. A cloth covered it with sun and moon symbols, and a tarot card deck and candle sat waiting on top.

"Let's sit," Lynn said. "Actually, it will feel good to sit down. I just got a new, large tattoo on my stomach yesterday, and I need to take it easy. It's itching like crazy."

Dawn glanced at the other woman's covered torso and wondered if it was polite to ask what sort of tattoo she'd gotten. Before she could decide, Lynn asked, "May I offer you some tea or water?"

"No thanks, I'm good," assured Dawn as she tentatively sat down at the table. Ignoring her, Lynn served her hot tea from a nearby earthenware teapot. Dawn shrugged and took the proffered cup. She took a sip of some sort of citrus and lavender tea blend.

"OK, let's talk," started Lynn, getting straight to business. "What brings you to me today?" She leaned forward so as not to miss a single word.

"I'd like to get a reading from you."

"Ah, but the big question is—why do you want to get a reading?" asked Lynn, cocking her head and raising her eyebrows, all with an encouraging smile.

Dawn found her gaze disconcerting. It was as if she already knew all of Dawn's secrets. Dawn had never experienced anything like this, but, being Dawn, she straightened her shoulders and look right back into those ice blue eyes. "There are things happening in my life, and I don't understand why."

"Good. Because you're not supposed to." Lynn beamed at her. "You are having a tremendous struggle right now around your identity. You're asking yourself, 'Who am I? What am I?' Is that right?"

Dawn nodded, surprised.

"Yes, good," said Lynn, clapping her hands. "Say more about that."

Dawn leaned forward and said softly, "It's hard to describe how I've been feeling, but I seem to have forgotten how to be happy."

Dawn surprised herself at her own words. She didn't expect to confide in Lynn, and yet here she was as if it were the most natural thing in the world. She went on, "I don't have enough life. I wish I was someone else. I think I lost my chance to feel good about my life, to be who I want to be. I mean, I have a good life, mostly. I have financial success and the best friends you can imagine. My girlfriends and I call ourselves the Gumbeaux Sistahs because we love each other like sisters, and we are all crazy about gumbo."

"Oh yeah? I love that! And I'm crazy about gumbo too," said Lynn. "But go on,"

"I am a widow with two children, and I've had to deal with that, and I'll admit it's been pretty hard." She glanced at Lynn's face and thought she saw a tiny glint of something register in her eyes. She went on, "But it's been a couple of years since my husband passed, and I think I'm learning to live with it, but I still feel like something's missing. But I'm not sure what. And I don't know which way to turn, Lynn." She lifted her hands in a gesture of frustration.

Lynn prompted her, "And this has you questioning your identity?"

"I thought I knew who I was pretty well by now."

"Well, you're obviously a strong woman with a strong personality. I can tell. But our personalities are subjected to many changes and challenges in our lives. And maybe our core values stay the same, but they still have to react to the changes in our lives, leaving us a bit stunned and free-falling at times."

Dawn interjected, "And then there's those damned crows!"

Lynn's eyes widened. "Excuse me?"

"Crows are following me! And cawing at me. One was even calling to me in your front yard just now!"

"Oh my! This is getting more and more interesting. Tell me about them."

"They're everywhere! They won't leave me alone. They wake me up in the morning with all their cawing at my window. They swoop at me in my garden. They drop feathers on me. It's crazy!"

"Oh my God," exclaimed Lynn, grinning wide. "That's fantastic!"

"Is it?" asked Dawn. "To me it seems like a horror movie most of the time. I don't know whether to feel scared or blessed."

"Oh, feel blessed, by all means! Very blessed."

Dawn went on, "My friend Helen says it might have to do with my spiritual wellness. That the crows are messengers of God, and that he or she is calling me."

"Your friend is right on the button. They can also be a symbol of death or loss or great change, but they're mostly good news. They represent the spirit world, and you can expect some big challenges coming your way. And some joy to go along with that too. The crows don't come to everyone. This is special, and you should feel honored. And you need to be both watchful and get into action. You might even need to travel."

Dawn perked up and grabbed the opportunity to ask, "You mentioned that you were on a spiritual trip out in California, I thought I would ask you about it."

"Of course. And it makes sense for you to ask. The crows and your recent identity concerns are all the same problem. They are all crises of a spiritual nature."

"You think so?"

"Definitely," confirmed Lynn.

An idea came to Dawn, and she hesitated to ask, but then blurted, "Do you think I need to go on a spiritual journey too?"

"Of course," said Lynn, smiling brightly.

"I wouldn't know where to go or what to do. Can you share a bit with me about your journey?"

"Now, that's a story all by itself," hooted Lynn. "But sure. I'll give you the highlights. This is actually the second time I've done this particular journey, except this time I'm taking the same trip by myself."

Dawn's ears perked up while her face fell.

Lynn went on, "When I went last time, years ago, we had an unforgettable trip. It was everything you'd want out of meaningful journey. We learned so much about ourselves on that trip."

Dawn prodded, pushing the point, "It must have been nice to have a romantic companion as you traveled. Am I right?"

Lynn ignored her question. "Like I said, it was a remarkable journey."

Dawn was disappointed and determined to ask Lynn more about Dan, but she didn't want to arouse suspicions. So she asked, "How did you plan your trip? How did you know where to go?"

"Ooh, girl, have I got the perfect gift for you." Lynn pushed herself up from the couch and padded gracefully over to a tall bookshelf. She took a small book from a low shelf and then walked back and put it into Dawn's hands. "This is all you need for your trip," she said confidently.

Dawn studied the book in her hand.

Lynn explained, "This book is amazing. It's a compilation of many spiritual locations to visit including retreats, monasteries, and abbeys."

Dawn glanced at the table of contents and saw that the information was organized by state.

Lynn enthused, "There are so many great locations in there. I've only been to about half of them so far."

"Good Lord," said Dawn, impressed, "Where do you even start?"

"Years ago, we wanted to cover the southwest, so we began in California." Lynn narrowed her eyes, watching Dawn's face.

Dawn gulped. Lynn was talking about Dan, and it was hard to swallow. Dan in California without her. *I can't believe he never told me any of this.* She felt deeply sad as well as astounded.

"We started out in Santa Barbara. We actually split up for a little bit as I made a couple of overnight side trips alone because the locations were for women only. One of those was in Merced, California. There's a group of Native American women there that hold sweat lodges. I went back there this time too."

"Sweat lodge?" asked Dawn. "Doesn't sound very inviting. In Louisiana, we avoid sweating as much as possible," she joked, but Lynn was serious.

"A sweat lodge is just what you need, but you have to be with people who know what they are doing. Some Native American tribes build these low-lying huts with branches, skins, fabrics, all natural materials, for a kind of an intense steam bath. It's a purification ceremony and the perfect way to start a spiritual journey. It's an honor to be included in such a ceremony. If you go on a trip, you should start there. It's not included in that book, so I'll have to text you their contact info. They know me, and I'm sure they'll allow you to come."

"Well, OK, but," started Dawn, "What else can you tell me about what to expect?"

"I'm not going to tell you too much," Lynn said firmly. "I want you to have your own experiences in these places. And they are such wonderful places. Don't worry, I'll text you my whole list of them. It's up to you to go to one or all of them. You can't go wrong. But now, let's get to that reading of yours."

She reached out and lit a large candle on the table. Then she picked up a well-worn Tarot deck and handed it to Dawn. "Here. Hold these for a moment and get your energy into them. Do you have a special question to ask today or do you want a general reading?"

Dawn thought a moment and decided, "Let's do the general reading today. I think it will help me focus."

"Good call," answered Lynn, nodding. "I also pulled a quick astrological chart for you and we'll get some things from that today. Now I want you to shuffle the cards a few times and cut them in any way you want. And then form them back into one deck for me."

Dawn did as she asked then handed the deck back to Lynn who started laying them out in formation.

"Looking at your Tarot reading, I can tell you spend a lot of time alone. You do, from time to time, feel lonely. There's a desire to reach out and call somebody and go do something, and when you get to that point, you are extremely needy. You're looking for someone else to fill your cup. You say, 'Go with me so I'll feel better.' When that happens, you need to do something just for yourself. We need to fill up our own cups and make ourselves happy. A friend of mine just cancelled some plans with me and she said to me, 'I hope you are not disappointed.' And I said, 'Of course not. My cup is pressed down and running over.' My life was not contingent on those plans. I have many things that I do to make myself happy. One thing I like to do is get in the shower or tub and wrap my arms around myself and rock back and forth, and giving myself love. I give my arms little kisses." She made kissing noises and kissed her arms and hands, laughing.

Dawn grinned and said, "Lynn, you are so funny."

"My ex-husband Joe used to say, 'Damn it, Lynn, you are crazy as a loon!'"

"Oh, you were married?"

"Oh yes, but that was so long ago I don't even remember. I do remember that back then, when he would say something like that to me, I would try to defend myself, or backtrack just to get along with him. But then one day, I just came to my senses and told him, 'You're right, Joe. I'm that and many other things.' It's hard to fight with that."

Dawn chuckled as Lynn said, "Let's get back to your cards. I see that you do need to keep your own counsel and not tell everyone every plan. Just go do it. Gather your strength and go do it. People will not always agree with you and it doesn't matter. People are always trying to tell us what to do," said Lynn, "And sometimes they are full of crap.

"Right now I know you are not happy or content with yourself. But look—you have three Tarot cups standing. They're not falling over; they are full. So, you are supported in your life. But if you are sitting there thinking, 'I can't do this. Shit, I'm scared!' then take fear with you on your journey. Just make sure you go anyway.

"A question you need to be habitually asking yourself is 'am I having fun?' Because honey, if you're not having fun in the second half of your life, after all you've been through and all the trudging, rowing, and going on and on, trying to make it in this world, then there's something radically wrong with what you are doing.

"Look, here's the Page card. The Page is a newbie and doesn't know the time of day. He's not the king and he's not the queen. He's brand new to the court and so are you in this phase of your life. See, he's only got this one wand that he's holding onto for dear life. This experience is going to teach you whatever it takes to make you comfortable at the court. The Page is trying to be strong and struggling to be centered. Now he really is all these things, strong and centered, but he has no mastery. Dawn, you feel you are the Page, but you are actually the Queen and she is already powerful.

"And now here's the Magician card. Notice the tools on the table. He's got the sword, the cup the wand and the pentacle—all of the powers he needs. He's got them all. And so do you. Also, you have a fine imagination. Notice the snake belt around the Magician's middle. The snake is wisdom. His baton is reaching up to the heavens, and he is saying, 'I'm reaching for the highest part of myself.' The Magician calls on his wisdom. He is pointing with his other hand to the earth and says, "I'm going to stand steady, feet firmly on Terra Firma with myself and Mother Earth.

"The cards are also saying that you need to open yourself up to every kind of fluctuation and change right now. And I have to tell you that with the fixed planets that you have, it's not going to be the easiest task for you. Because you like sureness. You like to know what's coming next. And that's fine. But for now, open, open, open up!

"Here's what I think. You should study the Tarot. It will help you. You're introspective in many ways. Your mind is penetrating. You are highly intuitive and have the ability to sit with someone and know if you are hearing the truth or know if it is plain old cock n' bull. You have an analytical mind, and you are a pioneer. I can tell that you have magnificent psychic ability."

Dawn gasped. Lynn paused, watching her closely. "What is it, Dawn?"

"That thing you just said—did you mean it? About my having psychic ability?"

"Of course I did," answered Lynn carefully, narrowing her eyes at Dawn. "But you already knew that, didn't you?"

Dawn felt her face redden, and tears nearly came to her eyes. "Lynn, I've never told anyone this before, but I feel like I need to tell you. I used to have visions of things when I was a kid." And just like that, Dawn's secret was out. She went on, "I never quite understood what they were but they helped me feel better when I was going through something hard. As I've grown older, I still get flashes of those visions, little ones that sometimes tell me something about a person or a situation. I never really knew what to do with it. I've never told anyone about them either. If you think learning the Tarot would help me understand myself better, then I would love to learn it, but I wouldn't know where to begin."

"Yes, I do think it will help you, and I'll teach you. You'll come to me for a couple of lessons, and I'll give you a book you can study too. But let me ask you, Dawn. Do planets make you do anything?"

Dawn looked puzzled. "What do you mean?"

"Never mind. I'll tell you the answer. It's simply, 'No.' Do the astrological houses force you to act in a certain way? No. Does the retrograde Mercury create havoc in your life? No. I've lived through two hundred and seventeen retrograde Mercury's in my lifetime, and I'm still sitting here today breathing in and out. The same goes with the Tarot cards. Do they make you do anything? No, they don't. They are merely tools, but powerful ones. The same with the I Ching and other divination tools. I believe, and I'm not alone in saying this, that they help the reader access a kind of collective consciousness and bring forth guided revelations. Just wait and see. Just keep your heart open to what comes."

Dawn looked troubled, "But I don't trust being able to read the Tarot correctly."

"Then practice that trust. You have to practice your gifts. You don't have to memorize the Tarot. You have to practice."

"I don't have to memorize this? Whew! That's good!" said Dawn with relief. "I can't remember stuff from one day to the next."

Lynn looked at Dawn, studying her face and said suddenly, "You've got the prettiest dimples. Do your kids have those dimples too?"

"Yes, one of them does."

Lynn nodded. "I thought so. Well, did I answer all your questions?"

Startled at the other woman's abruptness, Dawn blinked and nodded. "I'm not sure. I—I guess we have for now."

"Great, let me walk you out, and I'll talk to you soon."

CHAPTER 6

Dawn sat in her car in front of Lynn's house feeling as if she'd just been through a hurricane and then tossed out into the street. *"What was that all about? She sure was in a hurry for me to leave."*

But even more than feeling rushed, she was overwhelmed by some of the things Lynn had told her. And by the things she had told Lynn. *"I told her about my visions! I can't believe I did that!"* she thought. And as she sat in the warm car, memories, long buried from her childhood, came back to her clear as day. She remembered that she had written about the incidents in an old diary from her teenage years, a diary which, she knew, sat in a personal keepsakes box that Dawn kept in the attic.

"I'll have to go look for it when I get home. I think it all might mean something," she thought.

Dawn thought about Lynn's tarot reading all the way home to Covington. Lake Ponchartrain was smooth as glass as she made the long haul across the bridge to the Northshore.

She certainly had a lot to think over. For one thing, there was still the question of what Dan was doing taking a trip with Lynn. What was that about? Were they lovers? Or friends? Why hadn't Dan told her? She meant to ask Lynn after the reading, but Lynn had rushed her out so quickly she had lost her chance. But she would see her again soon and try again.

Then there was Lynn herself. *"What an oddball!"* thought Dawn. She thought Lynn was quirky as can be, but there was so much more to the woman than just that. Dawn sensed a wisdom in those flashing blue eyes. And the things she had said to Dawn like *"You have psychic ability."* Dawn didn't know what to make of that. *"Did it have something to do with the visions I had?"* she wondered. She was glad Lynn had offered to give her tarot card lessons. She truly wanted to learn, and she would have an excuse to ask more questions about everything. Along with the book on spiritual places to visit, Lynn also had given Dawn a book about the Tarot to study before their first lesson. She told Dawn to start familiarizing herself with the cards and to try doing a Celtic Cross layout for herself. Dawn couldn't wait to get started.

And then there was the idea of taking a spiritual journey. Before Dawn could even get in her car, Lynn had texted her all of the places she might include on her trip. "It will change your life, Dawn," Lynn had insisted. *"Had that trip changed Dan?"* Dawn wondered. She was so curious to find out and to see where Lynn and Dan had visited all those years ago.

Halfway across the bridge, she told Siri to call Lola. Her friend picked up the phone as if she'd been waiting next to it to hear from Dawn. Because she had.

"Spill it," said Lola. "What happened?"

Dawn described everything that had happened at the meeting including how quirky but formidable Lynn was.

"So wait. You still don't know about Dan and Lynn?" asked Lola, frustrated.

"No, I really don't," sighed Dawn. "But I will be talking to her again."

"Meanwhile, looks like you have to take a trip!"

Dawn answered slowly, "Yeah. I guess you're right, Lola. I was just thinking that. I guess I do."

"Want me to go with you?"

"More than anything," said Dawn, and then she gave a worried sigh. "I'm nervous about this whole business. This is brand new territory for me, as you know. But I think I have to do this one alone."

"I figured as much but thought I'd offer anyway. But, if you go, you'd better call me every day. I'll be dying to know everything."

When they hung up the phone, Dawn thought, *"Oh my gravy! Dawn Berard Takes A Spiritual Journey—sounds like a movie. A movie about someone else's life—except that it's mine!"* She shook her head in disbelief and drove home to plan a trip.

CHAPTER 7

Visions

When Dawn arrived back at her house, she dropped her purse on the kitchen counter, poured herself a glass of red wine, and walked into the hall to pull down the attic stairs. She climbed up carefully so as not to spill, and pulled the light chain. Harsh white light fell on several boxes of Christmas ornaments and other odds and ends. After a couple of minutes, Dawn found the box she was looking for marked *Dawn's Keepsakes*.

She hauled the box downstairs to the dining room, sat on the floor, and lifted the top to find a load of memories. Right away, she found her old diary and opened it, the lock having been broken many years ago.

She hadn't written every day in it when she was young, but she did capture some important moments and memories. This included entries she was particularly looking for, ones she had nearly forgotten but were being dragged to the surface from events like the crows manifesting in her yard and her reading with Lynn. These entries were about the first times she had had visions as a child.

Dawn had to hold the diary close to her face to read her awful teenage handwriting. As she read the entries, a long forgotten memory surfaced and brought fresh astonishment.

She remembered it vividly. The year was 1966 and Dawn was only six when she woke up one morning in her twin bed at dawn. Her little sister, Trinity, was still asleep in her bed in the small room they shared. Dawn remembered snuggling down in her striped blanket with a feeling of security and warmth and then being suddenly jolted from that sleepiness in one life-changing moment. She bolted upright, wide awake, and sat staring at the wall on the opposite side of the room, right over her sleeping sister's bed. She stared, open-mouthed, and squinted, rubbing her eyes over and over trying to clear her vision because what she saw was nearly impossible to accept. She simply could not believe her own eyes.

The wall was painted a creamy beige and held no pictures or decorations of any sort except a small crucifix that her mother had hung by the door. It was usually a clean slate, but it was anything but that morning. A massive vision covered the entire wall, surrounding her sleeping sister. Amidst wispy, white clouds and a crisp blue sky, an extraordinarily beautiful creature looked down on Dawn in her little bed. She kept blinking and trying to figure out why her eyes seemed to be going crazy on her. She remembered thinking, *"It must be the way the light is coming through the curtains at the window."* But she knew it wasn't. Even a six year old can tell the difference between shadows and reflections and an angel floating over her sister's head.

Then the beautiful, luminous creature smiled at Dawn, confirming that it was definitely no trick of the curtains. It raised an arm and beckoned to her. As if that wasn't odd enough, Dawn found that she wasn't afraid. She was, in fact, incredibly joyous, even though she was usually a rather anxious little kid. A ghost story or horror movie could force her to sleep with her head under the covers for weeks at a time. But even at that young age, she knew an angel when she saw one. She also knew that God had His hand in this vision. She felt that He was calling to her through this beautiful creature. It was one of the most enthralling moments of her life. She felt, simply, love.

She slowly crept from under her covers, walked across the room, and reached out to the angel. But all she felt was a solid, cold wall. It neither surprised nor disappointed her. She just thought she would try to touch it, just in case it was there in the flesh. But she already knew that the angel was a vision. She also recognized the importance of the vision in her life, even at the age of six. She knelt down on the floor and watched the angel while she prayed and smiled back at her. Then, after a short time, maybe five minutes, the vision faded away into the growing light of day, and the wall became blank once more.

Dawn remembered running across the room and jumping on top of her sister, saying something like, "Trinity! There was an angel in the room! Right over your head! And it was beautiful—it smiled at me and there were birds flying around behind and. . ."

Trinity moaned, half asleep, and said crossly, "Don't wake me up."

"But really, Trinity, she was right here!"

"That's great. Go back to sleep," she had murmured.

Dawn remember that she had felt astounded, and embarrassed. "*She doesn't believe me,*" she thought. It never occurred to her that her sister or any of the family would not believe her about something as important as an angel. She didn't know whether to be angry or frustrated.

Still, she got up, washed and dressed, and tried again at breakfast. The family, Dawn's four siblings and mother and father, listened half-heartedly as they rushed through the weekday meal. She told them the incredible news; an angel had come to visit. She had been dumbstruck when they all started laughing at her.

She had shouted, "No wait. I'm not kidding." Unfortunately, her family was always kidding around. "I mean it! It's true!" she had insisted, tears coming into her eyes.

They smiled at her, and her mother told her to finish getting ready for school. Dawn could tell that they thought that she was cute with her little angel story. She thought that they would probably talk about her at the office and to their friends that day. It was apparent to them that she actually believed her story, and that made the whole incident all the better in their eyes. It had been unbelievably frustrating for Dawn. She did not want to be cute. She wanted to be believed.

That was the first vision that she remembered in her life and the first of the huge lessons she was to learn. She had been just a little girl in a big family and was treated as such. By exposing that she had seen something that no one else saw or believed in, she opened herself up to condescension and ridicule, and she didn't like it one bit. She hated being laughed at. She never mentioned that particular vision to her family again, nor to anyone else again for years. She never even mentioned it to her husband, Dan, while he was alive.

Dawn went nosing further into her old diary and found another entry after a few pages.

She remembered that while she never talked about her visions, she sure thought about them often over the years. She wondered about them constantly when she was young. It occurred to her that maybe angels only appeared to little kids, and that is why her family did not believe her. She wondered if the other kids around her at school were seeing angels too and if they couldn't talk about it to their families either. She wanted to talk about it badly. If other kids at school were seeing angels, Dawn wanted to find those kids.

So, one day at recess she tried to find out if her theory was true. But while she needed to know if other kids saw angels, she didn't want the kids at school laughing at her like her family had. So she had discreetly asked two other little girls on the swings if they had ever seen any angels. One told her that she had seen a statue of an angel in the church.

Dawn had asked, "No, I mean have you ever seen an angel move?"

"I've seen angels in the clouds, and they move," the second girl had replied.

Dawn had thought *"What's wrong with these kids? Don't they know the difference between an angel and a cloud?"* She remembered the sharp bite of frustration she had felt.

She realized that they had not seen any angels, at least not the same kind as she had. She didn't tell them what she had seen. She didn't tell anyone.

Much later, as an adult, it had occurred to Dawn that there were probably many people who, as children, had experienced wondrous visions or events like this, but had been silenced about them. She thought that she would love to interview a random group of people one day to find out if they remembered anything truly unusual, something they couldn't explain, happening to them as children. She believed that the adult mind gets so attuned to the physical world that it could not or would not grasp the possibility of a child's vision. She couldn't blame them, but more's the pity.

Dawn recalled that she had looked for that angel in her house every morning for as long as she lived in her parents' house. The angel appeared to her twice more in the same year, basically in the same way. It showed up in the early morning, smiling, and motioning to her to come to it. The visit was always accompanied by a feeling of amazing love and joy. Immediately afterwards, it always brought some sadness knowing that she couldn't share the amazing incident with anyone.

She remembered being anxious to find out more about the visions. They were frustrating and confusing to her. What did they mean? Was it like the three little children at Lourdes who saw the Virgin Mary? Mary had spoken to those children though. The angel had not spoken to Dawn, and she fervently wished it had because the silence was killing her. Was she supposed to do something? She wondered if it meant she was supposed to enter a religious order or dedicate her life to God in some way. She thought about going to talk to a nun or a priest or someone at her church or school, but she was afraid they would laugh at her too. Besides, she was unbelievably shy in those days, and if you grew up Catholic as she did, you know that nuns and priests can be a pretty mixed bag when it came to personalities. She'd known nuns as strict and sour as bad prunes. She remembered one old, tiny nun who liked to squeeze the students' hands as hard as she could. She'd known priests who had taken her into the school hallways and screamed bloody murder at her for laughing too much in class. Of course, she'd also known nuns who were the sweetest people in the world. Her piano teacher, Sister Mary Ann was sweeter than butter. You just never knew what you were going to get in a nun or priest. She didn't feel safe talking to them about what was happening to her.

Then one day at school, she received a brochure about the Maryknoll missionary nuns who traveled into exotic places, like Africa, to spread the word of God. She remembered with a smile thinking back then, *That's it. I'll become a missionary—a Maryknoll nun!* She had begun to picture herself in this role except, of course, she really had no idea how to be a nun. The nuns she knew were all teachers. She couldn't picture herself teaching, but she tried to keep an open mind. Alone in her room, she had wrapped a handkerchief around her forehead and neck and then draped a black veil over her head. She had walked around the room with her hands folded trying to think up a nun name for herself. Sister Veronica was in the running. Veronica was the woman who carefully wiped Jesus' face on the day of his crucifixion. The truth was, she just liked the name Veronica. In reality, Sister Mary Confusion was a more apt choice of names for her.

Around that same time, she had read a book about the martyrs in the church and the incredible sacrifices they had made for God. She had been taught that sacrificing for God could bring her closer to Him. So she began to make little sacrifices thinking that by getting closer to God, she might understand her angel visions and know what she was supposed to do. She gave up candy, and sometimes she would miss the ice cream truck on purpose. Then she began to sleep with hard cover books under her pillow at night and offered the discomfort up to God. None of it worked. She just got a sore head and less ice cream.

After a while, she gave up the sacrificing. She also gave up the idea of being a missionary in Africa. Growing up in middle-class America, she had been taught to be practical. Dawn was under the strong impression that she needed to grow up, get a job, get married, have a family, and live a regular life. It didn't occur to her that she could do anything out of the ordinary. No one had ever said those words to her. She did not feel like she had that kind of permission. She didn't believe that she could actually go traipsing around the world helping the poor and hungry. She didn't believe it, so she didn't do it. Isn't that how it usually works?

Besides, she really didn't want to be a nun. Africa sounded good, but the rest of it didn't look like a lot of fun. Besides, she liked boys an awful lot. Sitting in her living room, she realized with a laugh that she still did, actually.

Looking back now, it was easy for Dawn to see what the visions meant. She wasn't meant to be a nun. Not by a long shot. The visions were prophecies, the coming out, the showing of the way. They were definitely a gift from God, a gentle revealing to her that she had a gift—the gift of visions. There were to be dozens more visions in her early life, but she would never forget the first—the beckoning angel inviting her to believe.

The memories were so vivid for Dawn. Sitting there in her dining room with her diary, she was moved to tears over the memory of the beautiful vision. She recalled the painful way she had dealt with them. She tried to remember when she had stopped having visions and realized it had been about the time she'd lost her parents at a young age and basically became the caregiver for her young brothers and sister. Suddenly, she was also struck with two realizations. She now believed that her visions were messages, and if they were happening again in her life, she would pay more attention to them. Plus, she would go on that spiritual journey to learn more about herself. And she would bring a journal to document her trip along with old diary so she could remind herself that this was reality.

There were other entries in the diary to read, and Dawn spent the better part of the evening learning about herself and putting the long-ago pieces together.

Then she opened her laptop and plotted out her trip.

CHAPTER 8

Sistah Visions

Two days later, the Sistahs crowded around Dawn's kitchen island helping themselves to big servings of rich, brown gumbo and rice. Lola slathered a thick piece of French bread with butter and plunked it next to her bowl for dunking.

Dawn was an excellent cook, as were all of the Sistahs. They'd known each other long enough not to be too competitive about it, although the jury was still out on who made the best gumbo. The women dug in and gave the best compliments you can give a cook—those "oohs" and groans over that delicious first bite.

Helen topped off everyone's wine glasses before she dug into her bowl and said, "OK, Dawn. You got us here, happily I might add, but you said you had something to tell us. So…" She motioned for Dawn to start talking.

Dawn glanced around the table. She did have something to tell them. It was a secret, and it was big one. She made sure everyone had at least one glass of wine before she dove in because, unlike her gumbo, what she had to say might be a bit hard to swallow.

"OK," she started. "This might be a bit hard for you to believe…"

"I knew it!" yelled Lola, grinning. "You're pregnant!"

Sixty-three-year-old Dawn gave her an incredulous look. "I said 'hard to believe,' Lola. But it's not an out-and-out miracle."

Helen, Judith, and Lola giggled. Bea stepped in, as usual. "Now, sistahs. Let the woman talk. Clearly this is serious business."

The Sistahs settled down and started back on their gumbo. Every eye was trained on Dawn, waiting for her to speak.

She continued, "Alright, here goes. You know how I went to visit Lynn. And I already told you that I didn't find out much about her and Dan yet. You also know that Lynn and I decided that the crows meant something important and that I needed to pay attention and plan a trip like the one she and Dan took, one of a spiritual nature. And that I'll be leaving on that trip in a couple of days."

"Yes, go on," encouraged Bea.

"But there's something you don't know about all of this. While I was at Lynn's, and she was doing my reading, I suddenly remember something about my childhood and told Lynn about it. It's something I haven't told anyone about for about fifty years. I'd almost forgotten about it, and then it suddenly all came flooding back to me. I had written about it in an old diary of mine, which I found."

She plunked an old, red book with a lock on the table in front of them. "There's some things about it in here, but there's even more that I didn't write down. When I got back home from Lynn's, I went up to the attic and found this and read through the whole thing. And it blew my mind how I could have had these things happen to me, and then just go about my life as if they meant nothing.

"And now with all the crows following me and talking to Lynn, I know that they did mean something. Something huge I think. And I want, no I need for you to know about them."

"Dear Lord, I can't stand it anymore, Dawn!" shouted Lola, a spoonful of gumbo halfway to her mouth. "Just tell us already!"

"Alright, I will," Dawn said, looking around at each of her friends. "Sistahs, I have visions."

Lola lowered her spoon, gaped at her friend and said slowly, "Wow, you're right. You're being pregnant would be easier to believe."

CHAPTER 9

A Spiritual Journey

Lompoc, California. Dawn stepped off the plane and made her way through the uncrowded airport lobby to the car rental stands. After picking up the keys to the van she had reserved, she spent the next ten minutes getting adjusted to the big vehicle. She wanted to rent a van because there was a good chance that she would need to sleep in it on this trip in some of the out-of-the-way places she planned to visit, but the newness and size of it left her a little nervous.

Her level of anxiety over driving the new vehicle was overpowered by her excitement for the trip. *"I can't believe I'm really doing this. I'm actually on a spiritual journey!"* She knew it was one of those moments that would impact her life immensely. With that in mind she reached over into her big orange tote bag for her journal to make sure it was still there. Her plan was to record her trip and her thoughts, as her memory was not what it once was, and she wanted to remember it all. Every detail. She hoped she could get used to the habit of journaling.

She had planned to make many stops and meet many people along the way. The stops included a sweat lodge, a monastery, a yoga center, and a Buddhist retreat center. The first stop was in Lompoc. She had been invited through Lynn to a sweat lodge ceremony for women. It was being held on a tract of land owned by a woman named Rosemary from the Chumash tribe. Dawn followed Lynn's directions and drove the van down the main highway quite a ways, enjoying the scenery.

The dry, brown and gold Californian hills had a hypnotic effect on Dawn's thoughts, and she found herself drifting back to two nights ago when she had told the Sistahs about her visions for the first time.

Much to her surprise that night, except for initial astonishment and a big round of teasing by Lola, she finally made them realize that she was serious—that she had had numerous visions when she was younger. Then they simply bombarded her with questions.

"What are the visions like?"

"Can you make predictions?"

"Have you talked to the ghost of Paul Newman? Can you get him to visit?"

That last one was Lola, of course.

Then Helen said something she would never forget, "Dawn, the universe if conspiring to send you in a new direction. I'm so proud that you are paying attention and taking action. This will be a turning point in your life."

And Judith added, "Dawn, we'll support you a hundred percent on this."

Lola said, "Wow, do we call you Madame Dawn from now on? Dawn had been so grateful for their reactions and support. They were just as excited for what was going on in her life as she was. She knew she could count on them. She always could.

A sign on the California highway brought her back from her thoughts, and she saw her turnoff in Lompoc coming up. It was early evening when she pulled off onto an asphalt road that quickly turned into dirt.

There was no cell reception at this point, and Dawn could only pray she was going the right way. The road ended at a property with a wooden fence and open gate. Dawn could see a small, wooden house up a tree-lined driveway. Several women stood around on the front porch, so Dawn figured this had to be the place. She parked and walked up the driveway slowly. A woman broke away from the group and came to meet her. This was Rosemary, and she invited Dawn to join the group on the porch where she welcomed eight women, including Dawn, to the sweat lodge. Rosemary was in her forties, Native American, slim, brown, graceful, and beautiful. It was hard not to stare at her. She was ethereal and serene and seemed so at home in this natural setting. Dawn thought she could probably disappear into the woods and live as a nymph with no problem at all.

Many of the women brought tents, sleeping bags, and camping gear in order to spend the night in the woods. Dawn didn't come prepared with any of that, but planned to spend the night in the van she had rented and was thankful she had.

Dawn introduced herself to some of the other women in the group. There was Sandy, a blonde woman who right away let Dawn know that she had just undergone what she called a Sundance ceremony. It's a highly revered ceremony performed by some tribes where they pierce the skin around both sides of a person's collar bones and then lift them in the air by their bones. It was supposed to be a test and a blessing. Dawn was immediately and truly aghast, but tried not to show it. She realized, and it wouldn't be the last time on this trip, that she was not among her sistahs back home in Louisiana. She would meet people and learn things on this trip that were new and strange, but Dawn welcomed that. Dawn had seen a version of this ceremony done in a movie called *A Man Called Horse* years ago, but never realized that the ceremony was still performed in real life today. She was astounded to hear about it and a little horrified. However, there was a strong inner peace and strength that emanated from Sandy. Dawn was in awe of what the woman was willing to undergo in her spiritual quest.

Dawn then talked briefly with a woman named Angela who was from South America. Angela had a classic Mayan look to her, as if she had stepped right off of a relief from some ancient Aztec temple. She was beautiful and dark with roses in her skin. She was also a peaceful soul.

Dawn felt so lucky to find herself in such unusual company. She was a little embarrassed to introduce herself as an accountant firm retiree who now owned an art gallery. It didn't seem very interesting compared to these other women, but she told herself that if nothing else, they were all on unusual, important journeys, and that made them sisters in that experience.

Dawn noticed that a couple of the Native American women would not speak to her. They walked away when Dawn approached them to introduce herself. Rosemary told her later that the women would have nothing to do with white women. The land on which they were holding the sweat lodge was once a hiding place for the tribe when Native Americans were hunted and captured for slave labor in the area. The women were upholding a long tradition in the area to simply ban the white people from their universe as much as they possibly could. Obviously, Rosemary didn't go along with this tradition because she welcomed Dawn and two other white women into the sweat lodge.

Before the sweat lodge ceremony began, Rosemary had the women lay on the ground in the yard, flat on their backs, in a circle and told them to give and take energy from the earth. She said that Mother Earth healed them and was happy to share energy. Dawn had to admit that it felt wonderful to just have permission to lay right on the ground without a mat or anything underneath her. She felt the pine needles and sandy dirt under the beautiful evening sky. She could have stayed there for hours.

After the sun had gone down, at Rosemary's signal, the women converged in front of the sweat lodge. They were taught to greet the four directions, north, south, east and west, and then their ancestors before entering the lodge which had been prepared for them. The lodge was a very low-lying mound made roughly with branches and hides. Dawn had to open a hide flap and stoop to get in and then crawl around the edge of the lodge to make room for everyone coming in behind her to sit down. There was a pile of stones in the middle which had been heated in a nearby camp fire. The floor was dirt, and there were several small carpet pieces circling the stones to sit on.

When everyone was seated, the door flap was closed and inside the lodge was completely dark. Rosemary invited everyone to offer prayers for peace together and then to make their own prayer offerings. Water from a bucket was ladled over the hot stones so that steam would rise and purify the women. Occasionally, a stone would be added from someone outside of the tent to keep the temperature correct in the lodge. And in this case, correct meant that it felt like the middle of hell.

The effect was shocking. Dawn found it unbelievably hot and stifling, and the ceremony lasted for what felt like hours. Several women could not take the heat and had to be let out of the flap during the ceremony. Dawn herself was on the verge of passing out, but she so badly did not want to miss the experience. She also did not want to be thought of as old or weak or "not being able to take it." Fool that she was, she had always known that she was a proud person but until that night, she didn't realize how proud she was. She kept thinking that if Sandy could go through that horrifying ceremony, then she could bear a little heat. But she felt as if she might possibly die that night. She was suffocating. She knew that she could leave at any time and was constantly on the verge of doing so, but she kept saying to herself, *Just one more minute.*"

The women chanted and passed a lit pipe with tobacco in it. The smoke made the lodge even more unbearable. Dawn prayed for strength. She found herself leaning over in the dark and digging her hands into the earth because there was a slight coolness underneath the sandy soil. She was panting and sweating and afraid. Each time she started to ask to be let out of the lodge, something made her hold back again and again. Then just as she thought she could not stand it any longer, just as she started to black out, she felt a cool breeze on her face. And at that moment, she suddenly noticed a window behind her on the hide wall. There was light in the window and the breeze came in with the light. She put her nose as close to the window as possible, rubbing her face against the hides. She breathed in deeply and felt herself calming. Tears came and were flowing down her cheeks. She suddenly knew she would be alright.

At the close of the ceremony, the women exited one by one. They sat in silence for a while and shared cool drinks of water. Dawn came out of the lodge and welcomed the clean air on her skin. She tasted fresh water and had never felt so alive in her life. She was almost delirious with joy and life. Her mind was clear as a bell. Later, she walked around the sweat lodge, examining it from all sides. There were no breaks in the wall of the lodge. There were certainly no windows. She knew then that the lighted window had not been real. It had been a hallucination. A vision. One that might actually have saved her life.

Afterwards, the women shared a potluck feast together, and then the group split up little by little, climbing into sleeping bags and drifting off to sleep. Dawn climbed into the van and slept sweetly and thanked God for delivering her through the experience. She wrote for a moment in her journal and hoped fervently that the rest of her experiences on her journey would be as reviving, but maybe not so harrowing.

The next morning, breakfast was served and then a large celebration took place in honor of women of all ages. Many new women arrived, and everyone was wearing beautiful, colorful skirts. They gathered in an open field under a bower that was hand-made of branches and grass. It formed a large circle, and the women looked like bright flowers in a meadow.

Right before the celebration began, Dawn spoke with Rosemary and told her how she had hallucinated a window in the sweat lodge and felt that it had saved her life. Rosemary was amazed. She said that people sometimes had visions during the ceremonies, but that she had never heard of anything like that happening before. Then she said that it made sense because windows open when you find the way to Spirit. She told Dawn that Spirit had blessed her at the sweat lodge, and Dawn felt that it was the truth. She found herself thanking God during the celebration.

It was a wonderful, love-filled afternoon. The women were so colorful, and everyone was very happy to be there. They sat on the grass in their graceful skirts and took turns going around the circle talking about their thoughts on being a woman, exploring both the dark and the light, whether it was a young woman talking about being in love, or being raped, or an older crone talking about loss or the gratefulness for wisdom in a long life.

When Dawn drove away that afternoon she knew that she had been blessed to be invited and felt that she had also been given a sign that she was indeed on a spiritual journey and on a path to God.

From Dawn's Journal

I can't believe how lucky I am to be here in this place with these remarkable women and on this journey. It feels like it was a long time coming, and I didn't even know it. It's been wonderful so far. True, I almost died in the sweat lodge, but let's not let a little thing like that kill the buzz. I just hope fervently that the rest of my experiences on this journey will not be so in-my-face! But on we go. A window had been opened, and I will keep to the quest.

CHAPTER 10

"Lola, it's me."

"Woman, it's about time! I've been waiting to hear from you—and so has everyone else. Judith says to tell you that the gallery is fine and Bea and Ellen send their love. OK, got that out of the way—now start talking!"

Dawn felt pure delight to hear her friend's voice and couldn't help but laugh. "Lola, I have so much to tell you, and I don't have a single idea of where to begin. I spent last night in a van I rented like some old hippie! I buried myself in a sleeping bag. Can you believe it? I mean, when was the last time you knew me not to be comforted in anything less than five hundred thread count Egyptian cotton sheets?"

"Uh, never."

"But I slept like a baby doll! And when have you ever known me to keep a journal? A journal, for heaven's sake!"

"Never. And that's two for two."

"That's right, sistah. I'm doing new things with new people and doing my best to learn something about myself."

"What are you learning?" Lola asked with genuine curiosity.

"I've learned that I'm stubborn and too proud," Dawn said, thinking of how she held out from exiting the sweat lodge when she was suffering from the heat and claustrophobia.

"Oh, what a surprise," drolled Lola.

"I also learned that the mind is very creative all on its own," she said, thinking about how she had hallucinated a window as a means of comfort and survival.

"Plus, I learned that it's important to stay close to the earth. Nature is healing. And I learned to expect to receive and to give love to others. And to explore gratitude. And that woman are so powerful together."

"Holy smokes," said Lola, "You learned all that in one day? I have to admit that I'm impressed."

Dawn grinned, "I'm impressed myself, sistah. I'm so happy I came here."

She went on to describe more about the ceremony the night before and that afternoon.

"So, where are you heading next?" Lola asked.

"Rosemary put me in touch with this woman who lives in Merced who is holding a special Angel Event ceremony tonight. I'm heading there now."

"What in the world is an Angel Event?"

"Oh, who knows, but I'll find out."

"This is such an adventure, Dawn. I'm actually jealous."

"I know—it really is. And don't worry, I'll call you the morning after."

"Text me when you are going to call. I'll scoot over at that time to the gallery, and you can Facetime with all the Sistahs. Meanwhile, promise you'll be careful, OK?"

CHAPTER 11

Angel Time

Dawn's next stop was the Angel Woman's house in Merced, California. This stop was not in the book Lynn had given her or even in her original travel plan, but had been recommended by Rebecca at the sweat lodge. Fortunately, Dawn's schedule was just loose enough to include it.

She had called ahead and arranged to spend the night in her rented van again on the Angel Woman's property because the gathering would go late, and she had no idea how she would find her way back to a motel in the middle of the night. The Angel Woman also told Dawn that she could shower in her house come morning, for which she was grateful.

After reaching Merced, she drove down numerous country roads and arrived around dusk at an unpretentious little house in the middle of a collection of small horse ranches. She opened a swinging gate, as she had been instructed to do, drove through, and re-latched it behind her.

A middle-aged woman with long gray hair opened the front door and introduced herself as Alice, The Angel Woman. When Dawn stepped into the modest house, she looked around and stared in shock. Everywhere you looked, there were angels. They hung from the ceilings, adorned the walls, sat in corners, and covered every inch of the room. There were angel pictures, dolls, sculptures, fountains, and figurines. It was an amazing collection, really. There were so many things to look at that, at first, Dawn didn't notice that there was a half-dozen other women sitting in folding chairs amongst the angels. They actually startled her. They smiled at her in welcome.

They introduced themselves, and most of them were from nearby houses and neighborhoods. Dawn was the only one from out of state. She was the last to arrive, so the group immediately got up to move outside where they gathered around a huge stack of wood for a bonfire. They lit the fire, and the ceremonies began. They talked about life, blessings, and supporting each other. They sang songs long into the night, praising God and Spirit and asking angels to watch over them and intervene in their everyday lives.

The Angel Woman told the group how the angels talked with her every day and told her about events that would happen in the future. She went around the group and told everyone something about themselves that the angels were telling her. She told Dawn that she would find what she was looking for on her trip, and Dawn truly hoped she was right.

Then they sang as they watched the fire die out. It was a beautiful ceremony. Dawn loved looking at the stars and being with those loving women.

When it was over, she found her way back to the van and tried to get some sleep. Unfortunately, she was having a hard time of it. It was hard to get comfortable in the van. She couldn't lay out straight, and there was always some knob or chair arm poking her in the side. But her mood didn't dampen. The excitement of the trip carried her through the discomfort.

She dug out her old diary and a flashlight because she wanted to read about her vision experiences again. She found that they helped to remind her of why she was on this trip to begin with.

I was twelve. I was sitting on our front porch on a hot summer day. We had no air conditioning in the house at this time, and the porch was a good place to go in the heat. If you sat in the shade, skin touching the concrete, you could feel some of the retained coolness from the night before.

If you were twelve, you could even put your face against the concrete, as I did then.

I was laying there studying my arms.

"It's so strange," I thought and turned my hands over and over, staring at them.

My brother looked up from a porch chair where he was reading one of his science fiction books. "What is?" he asked.

I sat up, still looking at my arms.

"What are you doing?" he asked.

"Can you see through your arms?" I asked him.

He snorted. "Can I see through my arms? Oh wait, of course I can. And I can shoot laser beams through my eyes too," he laughed. He really did read too many science fiction books.

I laughed too, but I kept staring. "No really, can you? Can you sometimes see through people like they're kind of invisible, but not quite?"

He smirked at me. "Are you saying that you can?" He made his eyes go big and weird, making fun of me.

I ignored him and kept looking at my arms. "Sometimes I can," I said, "Sometimes if I look at people a certain way, they become partly invisible. And then I see their colors."

"Colors? What are you talking about?" he asked. He sounded disgusted.

"You know, the colors that people have." I looked up at him. I was getting annoyed myself. "You know, like sometimes you have an orange kind of halo around you. And sometimes it looks like you are turning kind of red, but not in the face." I made him look at me "What color am I?"

Now he was annoyed. He said, "You are the color stupid."

"I'm not being stupid. You're stupid. Just tell me, can you see through people or not." Now I was mad, but I really wanted to know.

"Of course not. And you can't either. Now quit being nuts and leave me alone. I'm trying to read here." He went back to his science fiction.

I went back to the real thing. I looked at my arms again and then back up to my brother who was engrossed in his reading.

That was a real awakening for me. Up until that moment, I thought that what I was sometimes seeing—transparent and opaque colors in people—was normal for everyone. I did not realize that other people could not see what I now know to be auras, the energy fields that exist around every living person.

It surprised me. It also angered me because once again, I had exposed myself to ridicule. I hated when my family said I was crazy, or worse, stupid. I was only a kid, but I had pride in myself and wanted some credit. Some respect. I sure as heck wasn't going to ask anyone else if they could see through arms again. It was just one more thing I couldn't talk about. I could see these things, that much was certain. And they couldn't. Now I knew. I also knew that people didn't like me when I brought things like this up in conversation. When would I ever learn? Just keep it to yourself. It was the same lesson, a different day.

◆◆◆◆◆

Dawn fell asleep in her van while reading the old diary, but at dawn, she awoke with a start. The entire van was shaking. She was startled, utterly confused, and she couldn't figure out what was happening. The last thing she remembered was reading her diary, and the next thing she knew, she was in her hippie van, and the darned thing was rocking and rolling. *"Earthquake!"* she thought, as a newbie Californian. She held still, but the shaking kept going for a long time. *"Too long for a bloody earthquake."* She sat up, suspicious, looked out the front window, and then laughed out loud. A large, brown horse was rubbing his nose, over and over, on her windshield. He was going after some invisible itch and was pushing the whole van around. Dawn watched him for a while, delighted, but then realized that the horse was actually also cleaning his nose on the window. It was smeared and truly disgusting.

She quickly got out of the car, steered clear of the horse, and headed to the house in order to shower and have coffee with Alice.

Dawn told Alice about the horse, and Alice almost fell over laughing. Afterwards, Dawn borrowed the Windex to clean off the windshield. The horse would just have to find himself another big Toyota tissue.

From Dawn's Journal

The Angel Woman spoke of consciousness and enlightenment as being the same thing as love. She spoke about how being able to view different perspectives of situations, seeing things through other's eyes, and holding them in love would elevate all of our consciousness. This resonates with my heart so much. And my heart needs healing. But I'm going to keep her words in mind throughout this trip. Perhaps it will allow me to open my eyes as well as my heart.

CHAPTER 12

"Hey Lynn, it's Dawn."

"Hey, girlfriend, how's the trip going?"

Lynn's jovial voice on the phone put Dawn in a frame of mind to share and laugh. She thought, "*She has such a good effect on me,*"

Dawn enjoyed talking to Lynn, and she also wanted to keep in touch because she still needed to know about Lynn and Dan's relationship. It was also because Lynn knew so much about the very journey she was on, and Dawn found it helpful to run things by her. She always had something insightful to comment about Dawn's experiences.

She ended up telling Lynn about the horse cleaning his nose on her windshield, and Lynn just lost it on her end. She was laughing so hard, she couldn't speak for a moment.

Dawn couldn't help but think that if this woman was anyone else but someone who may have been having an affair with her husband, she and the other sistahs would love to know her better. She could picture Lola and Lynn cutting up and laughing together. And she pictured Helen and Lynn talking about healing touch and essential oils. She sighed and put it out of her mind for a moment, and told Lynn that her next stop was the White Lotus.

"Get ready for some serious serenity," said Lynn. "I love that place. Wish I could share it with you."

Dawn was surprised because she felt he same way. Talking to Lynn both comforted her and confused her.

"I'll tell you everything when I get back."

"Take care of yourself, Dawn. And be careful."

"She sounds like Lola," thought Dawn. *"She sounds like a friend."*

CHAPTER 13

"Hey there, sistahs!" said Dawn into her phone. On the Facetime call was Lola, Bea, Helen, and Judith who were all yelling out Dawn's name and waving.

"How's it going, dear?" asked Bea with a happy smile.

"You look fabulous, Dawn," said Helen. "So healthy!"

Dawn bowed and preened for her callers, joking around. "Thank you. I feel healthy. I feel like my body and my soul are blossoming. It's hard to explain. Maybe it's just from the challenge of doing something new, but I think it's more than that. I feel very alive!"

"Tell us about last night's ceremony with the Angel Woman. What a great name she has, by the way!" said Judith.

Dawn told them about her evening, and the Sistahs listened, enraptured. But when she got to the part about the horse using her rental van as a handkerchief, the Sistahs erupted into laughter. Lola got the hiccups, she was laughing so hard, and Helen had to pat her on the back. She gasped for air and said, still laughing, "I guess he showed you what he thought of you!"

"Yeah, I'm guessing that the horse is not your spirit animal, Dawn," laughed Judith.

After catching her breath, Lola asked, "OK, so tell us what you learned from this latest adventure?"

"Hmmmm," thought Dawn. "I guess being out in the woods at night confirmed again how magical it is to be in nature. And singing together was powerful too. There's something about making sacred-sounding music that opens up the heart. We have to go out in the woods and do this when I get back."

Judith snorted with laughter. "This is Louisiana, Dawn. The woods here are full of mosquitoes and the waters have alligators. Can we manage it in a backyard?"

"I'm thinking Lola's yard is the perfect spot for us. The time and care she's put into her garden with the addition of the butterfly garden area are just filled with love and good intentions."

"Can we drink wine and eat gumbo afterwards?" asked Judith, joking.

"I'm not doing it if we can't," joked Dawn. "And speaking of being together with women friends—and I already knew this from hanging around you crazy people—but women are so powerful, energetically. You could just feel the energy crackle around that bonfire last night. I always thought that I had to be with good friends to feel any kind of bonding, but it's not true. Those women last night were total strangers to me, but we left feeling strongly connected. We even exchanged emails."

"Bring them all home with you, dear," smiled Bea. "We'll show them all a *bon temps* around a bonfire!"

"So, where are you heading next?" asked Helen.

"I'm on my way now back to Santa Barbara. I'll get there this afternoon, and I'll spend the night at the White Lotus Yoga Foundation. It's a yoga retreat center, and the pictures I've seen of it online look gorgeous."

"OK, well you know what I'm going to say—be careful, and call me tomorrow!"

"We miss you, Dawn!" hollered Helen.

Dawn smiled fondly at her friends. "Ditto sistahs!"

CHAPTER 14

White Lotus Yoga Foundation

The White Lotus was a yoga retreat house hidden in the hills outside of Santa Barbara by the Los Padres National Forest. Dawn drove up a long driveway in the van, in which she was feeling quite at home at this point. It was mid-morning, and she found the yoga studio to be beautiful, quiet, simple, and seemingly deserted. After wandering around the grounds for a couple of minutes, she let herself into the main building and called out, but no one answered. She waited, looking at photos on the walls of the organization founder doing some very difficult and painful-looking yoga poses. Dawn finally found a man named Sven, in a back office who showed her where she would be staying. He escorted her out the back door, down a short dirt road to a beautiful copse of live oaks. Nestled among the oaks were several small white yurts with little wooden porches. This was where Dawn was to sleep, and she was the only guest in this area that night. The setting was peaceful and completely quiet. Dawn was delighted.

Sven went back to his office and Dawn settled her belongings in her yurt and then headed back to the yoga studio. She was still alone, so she played some meditation music and mimicked, for her own amusement, the pretzel-like yoga poses posted all over the walls. She fell over a few times and laughed at her own foolishness. She could imagine her husband Dan trying the poses too while he was here, and she laughed at the idea. She wondered if he tried any of the classes or if he had stayed in a yurt too—and if he did, was he alone?

After a few more awkward falls she looked up to find a woman watching her from the doorway with an amused smile. Dawn jumped up, still laughing, and said, "Well, this is embarrassing."

"Not at all," said the strange women in a deep voice. "You're playing. It's fun, and we don't do enough of that. I think it's healthy. I'm Sondraya, by the way."

"I'm Dawn, it's nice to meet you, Sondraya."

To Dawn's surprise, the other woman plopped down on the floor next to her and said, "Here, let me show you how to do that last pose. In yoga, it's all about breath and form." She showed Dawn the pose as well as a couple more, and Dawn actually felt herself loosening up a bit.

Sondraya asked, "So what brings you here, Dawn?"

"Just visiting here from Louisiana. And you?"

"I'm visiting friends here at the White Lotus. I'm from Sedona, Arizona. I do healing work and psychic readings there, and this week, I'm doing a bit of a work and play visit. I'm heading back home tomorrow."

"Sedona? Really? A friend of mine is visiting there right now. It sounds like a place I might have to visit."

"Oh there's no question about that. You would love Sedona."

"So, you do readings? Do you have time to do one for me?" asked Dawn, hopefully.

Sondraya thought a moment and then said, "I do. Let me get my phone from my room so I can record your session, and I'll meet you back here in a bit, OK?"

Dawn was delighted. "Great!"

"And give me your birthdate, time, and city where you were born, and I'll work up a quick star chart for you too."

◆◆◆◆

A half hour later, Dawn and Sondraya sat in two comfortable chairs in the yoga studio, as Sondraya finished getting her phone ready to record.

"OK, ready?" she asked Dawn.

Dawn nodded excitedly.

Sondraya looked over her notes and began. "OK, in examining your astrological chart, I can see that about two years ago your spirit challenged you a lot. People were taken right out of your life. And there were a lot of shifts that occurred at one time. It was extremely difficult, and I hope that you claimed to yourself that only good can come out of those changes.

Dawn's eyes opened wide, and she immediately felt the tears well up. "I lost my husband about that time. Heart attack."

"I'm sorry for your loss, Dawn. Spirit knows I've had challenges too. Some worse than others. Losing a husband can be one of the worst. But listen, good can come out of any challenge, even a terrible one. Let me give you an example: one night, I was driving, and some guy came out of nowhere and smashed into my car, totaling it, and I quickly thought out loud in that moment, 'only good will come out of this!' Now, I had no health insurance at the time. It turned out the guy was very drunk, and because of it, I got a new car out of the whole thing. And my car was falling apart anyway. So it was perfect. And I know that if I hadn't claimed it from the universe, it might not have happened. The police helped me in ways that they don't normally do because I made that claim. It helped."

She reached out and took Dawn's hand, looking into her palm. She pointed to a spot in the middle. "Look here. These islands in your hand show a tendency—and it's not just you, it's many women on this planet—it shows we've been trained to sacrifice.

"But it's changing. The energy is changing. There is new energy on this planet that's never been here before. It's so immense. It's the same kind of energy when Buddha was able to come into life and when Christ walked the planet too. All these great ones have come to the planet during this kind of energy. The difference now is that it's not about one person. It's about the Christ and the Buddha and about all of us, too. The only thing I'm concerned about in the old teachings is that they got parts of it wrong. The traditional way of the Buddha teaches that it would take a person a long time to come to enlightenment."

She snapped her fingers loudly, startling Dawn. "But no, that's wrong! I mean it *can* happen that way, the traditional way through meditation, but it can also happen in a twinkling of an eye. I've worked with people now who have worked utter miracles. It can come in the twinkling of an eye. That is the promise to us—that we can be changed that quickly. I believe that those old teachings worked for a certain amount of time. But I say no to them now. And I say no to all outside teachings right now. And I'm not alone in this. We are supposed to get our teaching directly from within. Question everything, and claim your enlightenment. Right now, your main commitment should be to love. Meditate and love.

"And remember, the work gets done through the fun. I can attest to that. As we follow our hearts, we follow our fun. I'm saying that my life is really easy now, and I'm so joyful. But for a long time, I believed that I had sinned and had to atone for it. My life was very hard. But I threw that off my back. I said to God, 'I don't want to live like this.' I am not the same person sitting here today that sat here even a year ago or five years ago. So how am I responsible for her mistakes? Well, I'm not. And not only that, when I look back at her, I realize that she was a wonderful spirit, and she was always doing the best she could anyway. Listen to teachings, but question them. Take what works for you. And make them your own. We have to discern. We have to digest them."

She handed Dawn a tarot card deck and had her shuffle it and draw out three cards. "Look at the kind of card you have drawn here—the Queen. It's a mastery card where you have to take all the laws, everything you've ever learned about Spirit and use it. Make yourself and Spirit number one. So this is what you are learning now—to be strong, trusting that Spirit is in you and always gives you what you want and need. You just need to claim it and demand that it be so. Spirit can make the biggest changes in all of us. You're mastering your mind and what comes out of your mouth with your prayers. That's why you're here today, isn't it. That is what your visit here is about, am I right?"

"That's exactly right," said Dawn, tears forming in her eyes.

She looked at Dawn's hands again and went on. "Your teenage years weren't easy, were they?"

Dawn shook her head and admitted, "No. They were pretty challenging, in fact. My mom died and I took care of my younger brothers and sisters."

"But look, you've got these long fingers which mean you're always reaching. So for you, it's like loving that teenage aspect and bringing her into the light of who you are, so that side of you is honored and recognized. Because there's some very good points to our teenage side. Nature will protect you and make sure that no one walks over you. And that's what you're working with. To strengthen your love.

"And, you've got a lot of practical skills. A lot of fire too. There's a nice mixture of the elements in your chart. A lot of creativity. And a lot of good leadership skills. You're good at running a business too. You're going to be coming into your power now, a different power, and nothing will stop you.

"And you've got everything you need. Because you have very strong integrity and you have strong intention. Once you know what it is you want to do, there is no stopping you. You are flexible though, and that's good. It will help you in your work, but it has two sides. It's up to you to make sure that the positive side comes out. The negative side of it is that you give your power away. Someone can talk you out of something. So it's really important to stay centered in your heart and say, 'Spirit, open my heart. Let me know my heart and give me the strength to follow it. To do what I need to do.'

"You need to claim your strength. You need to wake everyday up and say, 'I claim the strength of God to run through my veins.' You call it and bring it into yourself."

Sondraya paused for a moment, looking thoughtful, before continuing, "You know, I had to claim it too. I'm a Pisces with a Cancer moon and used to walk around saying, 'God, I don't have any energy.' And I didn't. And doctors and astrologers couldn't tell me why. But finally I learned to say, 'God, give me energy! I need it!' What a difference it's made. It's changed my whole life. You *ask* for what you need. You say, 'God, make me aware of the strength you've already given me.' You do have the strength, but you also have your old habits and patterns. It's the habitual way you feel about yourself. Your habitual visions about yourself. Things that other people have told you about yourself that weren't true. You have to say 'no' to that. You throw it out and bring in to you what you truly wish. This is your time to do that. And you're ready. You command and demand it.

"You are a Scorpio/Cancer, Dawn—the mother. Look at your hand. This is your heart line. See how frayed it is. This is because of your water nature from Scorpio. You're very sensitive to the moods and desires of other people. You're always trying to meet other people's desire, and at the same time, you appear strong on the outside. But you're soft, and I mean that in a loving way. You've done this woman's thing, as I said, of giving your power away. In many ways, you know your truth and your desires, but if someone else has a need, you let go of your heart's desire to fill that need. It's imperative that you don't do that anymore. It's imperative that you do what *you* love. Your true presence is directing you through your heart. You can strengthen it yourself by speaking the words I've told you. By calling in and asking that all of yourself be full of light and life. And with your intention that you are going to follow your heart. Because your destiny is in your heart."

Sondraya looked at Dawn's palm again. "There's a square that's formed right here in your hand that means you have guardian angels.

You're really protected. All you have to do is call out because they are always around. And because it's a free choice universe, they can do a certain amount, but not much unless we ask them to. You need to demand and command and ask for what it is that you want and need.

"And it's obvious to me that you are intuitive and gifted in the ways of psychic vision. It's very strong in you. It's all there. Have you had many psychic experiences?"

There is was again. Someone telling her that she had psychic ability, first Lynn and now Sondraya. She hesitated a moment. She had told Lynn about her visions, but that was in response to Lynn seeing it in her palm. Sondraya was telling her it was there and asking her to share about it. She looked at Sondraya, who suddenly looked like a warrior queen and Dawn felt she could trust her. So she told Sondraya the story of the visions of her childhood and the intuitive moments that happened over and over in her life. It felt freeing to be able to tell another person about her truth. When she was finished, Sondraya took Dawn's hand in hers and said, "We are sisters in more ways than one, Dawn. I believe that you should come to see me in Sedona soon. You need to come to Sedona."

From Dawn's Journal

When Sondraya's reading was over, she hugged me tightly and texted me a recording of our reading together. I hated to say goodbye. I'd felt such a strong connection with her.

Afterwards, I went outside into the garden and sat alone for a long time thinking about the things that she had said. I was completely on fire. A shift had occurred during the reading. I knew that I had a lot of work to do. It would be my job now to heal my life through Spirit, put away my fears, and reach out to help others find joy, healing, and love. I would find my place in the world.

It was unreal to me that Sondraya recognized my gifts and helped me focus on manifesting what I would need in this new phase of my life.

And then a vision came to me sitting in that garden. While thrilling, it also brought calmness, and I welcomed it. I was sitting in a room at a table with other people. Angels hovered on the walls over the people, and I could hear sweet music playing. In the vision I held the hands of the other people in the room and the joy that pervaded from the touch raced up my spine. I wanted to sit with that vision forever. Tears of happiness were rolling down my cheeks. I knew I was seeing my gifts in use in the future. The joy that it would bring to me and others was miraculous. I felt ridiculously, wonderfully happy.

Later that evening I went out to find some dinner then made my way back to the yoga center and into my little yurt. Then the wind picked up and howled down the canyon, bowing tree branches all over the woods. The rain came up suddenly and worsened as the evening wore on. I hadn't seen a storm like this since leaving Louisiana. I huddled in my yurt.

We lost power, and I spent the night in the dark, wrapped in blankets, scared, alone, and awake most of the time while the storm beat down outside.

I prayed for God to keep me safe. Also, as per Sondraya's instructions, I prayed, commanded, and demanded that God show me what I need to learn about the universe and how to help people. I asked God to help me to not be afraid of this storm or of my upcoming life and challenges and to have confidence that I could actually help people. I'm anxious to get on with my journey and could hardly wait till morning. The storm is supposed to clear up early and the van is already mostly packed. I plan to leave at first light. I am so ready for the next step.

CHAPTER 15

"I'm a yogi!" announced Dawn, laughing on the phone with Lola.

"Yeah right," answered Lola, and Dawn could almost hear her eyes rolling through the phone. "Maybe Yogi Bear!"

Dawn chuckled. "You're probably right, Lola."

"OK, tell me the latest."

"Oh my gravy, Lola. I just spent the night in the most beautiful spot—in a yurt of all things! In the middle of a national forest. And a storm came up and the wind was terrifying. If I had been back home, I would have sworn it was a tornado. Then it absolutely poured, and the power went out. It was quite the night. But it was all over in the morning, and yesterday I met the most wonderful woman up at the yoga studio. She was a woman our age named Sondraya, and she came into the studio just as I was making a fool out of myself trying to do some yoga exercises."

"Oh, I would have loved to have seen that!" chuckled Lola.

"She saw I was having trouble and offered to show me a couple of poses to do, so I got on the floor with her. It wasn't too hard, and she told me how the practice can improve the quality of and prolong our lives. It's kind of like a physical meditation. It relaxes you and creates energy flow in the body and lets us create more space in our mind for consciousness." She stopped for a moment, marveling at herself. "Would you listen to me? I'm telling you, things are changing for me! At any rate, I'm convinced we need to start doing this."

Lola sighed. "Oh lord, first we have to meditate, and now we have to do yoga. What's next? Singing Kumbaya around a campfire?"

"Don't knock it, sistah," answered Dawn, then added with a laugh, "And anyway, in our case, we would have to be singing Kumba-Ya-Ya!"

The two friends laughed easily together, and as usual, Dawn felt great affection and gratitude for her friend.

"But then, you'll never guess what happened. Sondraya told me that she is a reader, like Lynn, and offered to look at my palm and do a reading for me that afternoon. You should see her, Lola. I've never seen anyone who looked so cool. She wears all these wild, colorful flowy clothes, and she's so interesting. I could have listened to her all day. And guess what she said."

"I can't imagine," answered Lola. "Nothing would surprise me at this point."

"She told me that I had psychic abilities. That I had natural gifts for it. That's the same thing Lynn said to me. Sondraya advised me on how to manifest it, and she told me that I needed to go to God for what I needed. I'm so excited about all this, Lola, I don't know what to do with myself. And that's not all. Remember how I told you that one of the main stops on Lynn and Dan's trip was Sedona, Arizona? And that Lynn was visiting Sedona just this week? Well, Sondraya lives there! And she told me that I needed to make my way to Sedona and that when I did that I should look her up for a proper reading. Can you believe it? Sedona again! It's a recurring theme. I seriously think I'm going to have to make a second trip and go there. I feel it calling me. I'd go from here but I've got a couple of appointments to keep back in Covington, and besides, I already bought by plane tickets home. So, I'll come home and regroup then head on to Arizona."

"That sounds like a good idea. And Dawn, I can't help but being excited for you. I feel like you're out there learning things for all of us."

"That's exactly how I feel too. I will bring back home what I learn to share with the Sistahs. All I ask is that everyone stay open-minded because I think there's a lot to learn, and it feels like it's about to get wild in this universe!"

"Something tells me you won't have any problem with that in this group," chuckled Lola.

"Yeah, probably not," laughed Dawn.

"So, what's next?" asked Lola.

"I'm heading down to the Prince of Peace Abbey in Oceanside, California. The book Lynn gave me describes this place as being on a hilltop overlooking the Pacific Ocean, and it's run by monks. This should be interesting, right? I'll spend two nights there, and while I'm there I thought I might take a break from my spiritualizing and drive across the border into Mexico since I've never been there. It might make a fun day trip."

"Oh boy, OK. But you know what I'm going to say next, right?

"To be careful, and call you tomorrow?"

"You're a quick study, old friend. And listen, you may be a yogi, but I'm sorry, you are no monk!"

CHAPTER 16

Prince of Peace Abbey

Dawn's next stop was the Prince of Peace Abbey, a Benedictine monastery in Oceanside, California. The compound was old, mission-style, and housed many monks on a beautiful hillside. Dawn was shown to her room by a kindly faced monk who helped her with her embarrassingly over-stuffed suitcase. She felt foolish hauling in so much stuff to such a monastic setting, but the deed was done. She had never been any good at packing.

The room was perfectly monastic—spartan, even. It held a simple twin bed, a small wooden desk, and a crucifix on the wall. The city noise did not reach through the monastery walls, and it was quiet as a church. Dawn loved it immediately.

There was a *No Talking* rule at the abbey. The monk who welcomed her was allowed to tell her where she would stay, where she would eat, and the rules of the monastery, but then he left her alone in her room. There had been hardly anyone to talk to at the White Lotus Center either except for her short time with Sondraya. Noting this pattern, she understood that while silence was being required of her on this leg of her trip, she hoped she would get to talk to people soon. She had never been the strong, silent type.

The abbey provided very inexpensive accommodations for people who needed a spiritual retreat, and Dawn felt that described her to a tee. But once she settled in, she wasn't really sure what to do with herself, so she spent it visiting the stations of the cross in the abbey garden, reading in her room, and then driving into town to walk on the long Oceanside pier. She also visited a Rosicrucian temple that was located up the road from the monastery. She had never heard of the Rosicrucians before, so she was curious and drove up the narrow road to the pretty temple. She was even more curious about them once she parked the van and quietly entered the temple. The signs of the zodiac were painted in a circle on the ceiling. She wondered what that was about. She noted that there was a meeting to be held that night that was supposed to explain their beliefs to newcomers, and she decided to attend.

Once back at the abbey, she found that the monks were baking the daily bread which they sold to the public. She could smell the heavenly aroma all over the grounds, and it made her mouth water. As directed, she lined up for the evening meal that the monks provided, and they served her some of the bread with a stew. It was appropriately heavenly. The whole monastic compound was impressive. Everything slowed down at the abbey, and Dawn couldn't help but notice her own thoughts and feelings. She decided that she'd be a good monk, except that she would probably be in trouble often. She would eat all the bread and talk way too much. It would, no doubt, turn into one of those *How do solve a problem like Maria* situations.

That evening, she went to the Rosicrucian meeting, but didn't find that it shed much light on who they were and why the astrological signs were there. Instead, they talked about bringing in the harvest of one's life. It was interesting, but didn't satisfy Dawn's curiosity enough. So she googled them afterwards and found this description.

"Rosicrucian teachings are a combination of occultism and other religious beliefs and practices, including *Hermeticism, mysticism, and Christian gnosticism. The central feature of Rosicrucianism is the belief that its members possess secret wisdom that was handed down to them from ancient times."*

Dawn wished she knew what that secret wisdom was. She felt she could use some of it right about now. Still, while she found it interesting, she didn't really want to involve herself with any sort of religion. She wanted to go to the heart of God, to Spirit.

She went back to the abbey in time for the evening prayers which were sung in the church and echoed throughout the grounds. Dawn sat on a little bench in the chilly garden with a rough blanket wrapped around her shoulders. The stars were enormous in the sky and the deep voices of the singing monks were magical. She was there for almost an hour, utterly bewitched and thinking she was a very lucky woman to be experiencing that level of beauty.

The next day Dawn took a little detour on her spiritual quest to do some shopping. Yes, shopping. She couldn't help it. She was so close to the Mexican border that she decided to drive over and buy some trip souvenirs and Christmas presents, even though it was only September. She hoped to find unique gifts, and that it might even save her a bunch of money come December.

Dawn had never driven in Mexico before and was definitely nervous. The traffic was daunting trying to cross the border and even worse coming back into the U.S. She followed the signs that pointed to the "Mercado," or market, and hoped for the best. She got lucky and ended up wandering around for a couple of hours between many stalls of beautiful crafts. She chose gorgeous, woven blankets, silver bracelets, pottery, and a bull whip for Helen's son, Cooper. She knew he would like it, but hoped he wouldn't "shoot his eye out," as the movie line goes. She enjoyed practicing her broken, bad high school Spanish with the polite and patient vendors and was happy to find such unique gifts.

On the way back out of Mexico, she had her windshield cleaned a half dozen times by children in the street. Dawn tipped them all coins for the service, needed or not, trying to play the good guest in a host country.

When she got back to the abbey, she hauled all of her purchases back into her room so that she could repackage them for her continuing trip. She was making an attempt to keep the van neat as she went since she might have to sleep in it again. The abbot crossed her path as she struggled with her shopping bags heading back to the room.

"Having a productive spiritual journey, I see," he said, frowning with obvious disapproval.

Dawn's cheeks flamed in embarrassment, and once back in the room, she got miffed. *"Damned right I am,"* she muttered to herself. But it made her think, *"Am I really? I mean, what am I doing, what am I looking for?"* She knew she was looking for a spiritual awakening of some sort, but she really had no idea how to go about it. Getting in her car to visit and experience spiritual sites was all she had known to do. She didn't think shopping for her friends along the way was forbidden, but maybe she was wrong. She was making it up as she went along because the universe forgot to send her the Rule Book.

The next morning, Dawn decided that she had had enough of the silent abbey and was on her way again right after breakfast. She laughed to herself and thought, "That old abbot is going to have to find some other traveler to pick on now. Besides, I think I could take him." However annoying he was, the abbot had actually done her a service. He had focused the trip for her. It was definitely a spiritual journey she was on—nothing short of that.

From Dawn's Journal

I may not know exactly what I'm doing here, but I will have to trust that I will find my way, since I was so drawn to do all this. It may seem ridiculous, but that's the way it's going to be for now. I will pray that God will simply guide me on my quest. I will ask Him to help me learn what it is I'm supposed to learn. I told Him that it was very important to me, and that I was clueless and in His hands. I have faith that He'll help me.

CHAPTER 17

"Well, I got myself in trouble, Lola," sighed Dawn.

Lola chuckled, "That's my girl. That didn't take you long. What did you do now?"

Dawn told her about the monk giving her the stink eye over all her shopping bags at the monastery.

"Hmmm," she said thoughtfully. "Was he right?"

Surprised, Dawn mumbled, "I don't know for sure. It seemed innocent enough. I just wanted to bring everyone back something from my trip while I had the chance."

"Did you get everyone something? I mean, did you finish your shopping?"

"I did, actually. In fact, I just dropped a box of my purchases off at the post office so I wouldn't have to bring them on the plane with me."

"Well, good," said Lola with approval. "Look, I know you love to shop. Shoot, so do I! But why don't you give yourself permission to just not do that very much for the rest of your trip? You seem to be feeling guilty about it, and I think you should listen to that. Why not just concentrate on what you're there to do?"

Dawn was quiet for a minute then said, "Well, look at you being all wise and everything!"

"Yep, that's me." Lola grinned into the phone.

"I think you just might be right, sistah. And that was a good lesson. That materialism can get in the way of a spiritual journey. A good lesson indeed. The only shopping I'll do from now on is to buy beads and charms for a necklace I'd like to create for myself to remind me of this journey. It would mean a lot to me."

"Well that seems fine," said Lola, trying to support her friend. "And that shouldn't take up too much of your time."

Dawn went on, "Here's another lesson. I learned that spiritual music can transport you, especially under a star-filled night sky. I never felt as blessed as when I was listening to those monks sing like angels."

"Those sound like good lessons for us all. So, where are you heading next?"

"I'm on my way out into the Mojave desert to the town of Joshua Tree. Then onto the Vipassana Buddhist Retreat."

"Wow, that's gonna be interesting. I'll want to hear all about it, of course. Call me—a lot!" she laughed.

"You bet," laughed Dawn. "And before you say it, yes, I'll be careful."

CHAPTER 18

Joshua Tree

awn drove the van to Joshua Tree National Monument in the middle of the Mojave Desert. The monument is actually a huge park packed full of Joshua trees, a strange looking plant related to the cactus with spiky limbs pointing out in all directions atop a spindly trunk. They grow very tall, some as high as some saguaros. There is a prehistoric vibe to the trees, and Dawn's imagination had giant dinosaur lizards living amongst the roots.

She pulled into the parking lot at the monument with the intent to eat a picnic lunch and view the rock formations.

It was scorching hot so when she got out of the car, she popped up the sky light in the van to keep the car a little cooler. Then she put on her new Aussie hat with its raised side to protect her face from the beating sun. She also wore some khaki shorts and shirt with hiking boots and carried a walking stick, her lunch, and a drink-cooling tumbler full of ice tea.

She walked a good ways on a dirt trail and then found herself in the middle of a small, outdoor amphitheater nestled between some beautiful, huge boulders that looked like sleeping giants. According to a sign at the theater, nature talks were sometimes given there by park rangers. She noticed that there was, in fact, to be some sort of talk shortly and several people were already seated on stone benches and waiting. Then, something odd happened. When the people in the audience saw Dawn enter, they took one look at her Aussie hat and khaki outfit and assumed that she was the ranger. They started asking her all sorts of questions: Was she going to start the talk soon? What was the name of such and such a bird? What kind of rock was this?

Dawn was confused at first and then realized what was happening and thought the whole situation was pretty funny. Feeling a little mischievous, she got a "bee in her bonnet" and came up with a spur-of-the-moment idea. She didn't know where in the world the notion came from, but she suddenly found herself walking to the front podium. Keeping a straight face she said, "Hello, Ladies and Gentlemen, my name is Dawn, and I will be your lecturer today. Today's topic is not what is on the schedule. Instead I thought you'd like to discuss something that is of interest to us all—one of nature's greatest topics, in fact. Today I'm going to tell you about the birds and the bees."

She stopped and looked around. Some of the people were listening to her attentively and seriously, but a few had caught onto her joke and started to smile and even laugh a little. At that point, she couldn't keep the pretense up and broke down laughing. "OK, no, I'm just kidding you. I'm not a ranger, and I don't know squat about this place and couldn't give you a lecture if I wanted to. I'm only a visitor just like you. But that was fun, wasn't it?"

One man in the back yelled out, teasing, "Oh c'mon, tell us about the birds and bees."

She grinned at him and yelled back, "Well, no, there's no way that's going to happen, but y'all have yourselves a nice day!" She took a bow and walked off the stage. The audience laughed and some even clapped.

She walked away laughing. *What in the world got into me?* she thought, shaking her head at her own crazy chutzpah. She couldn't wait to tell Lola about this one. She then remembered that she was supposed to be on a spiritual journey and realized the lesson of the moment. It was the blessing of being able to laugh with others. It felt wonderful and it made them all feel closer somehow to each other. She hoped to do much more of it on her trip and in her life.

She started looking around for a good spot to each lunch and found a nice boulder in the shade where she could watch a mountain climbing group nearby giving lessons to a student.

Afterwards, she hiked up a hill and climbed to the top of a pile of boulders. There, she greeted the four directions like she learned to do at the sweat lodge, and thanked God for her life, her children, and her quest.

It wasn't until she got back to the car that panic struck. She realized that she had locked the keys inside the car. It was dangerously hot, and she was out of tea in the tumbler. Also, there were no cars left in the parking lot. She wasn't sure how to get help and was genuinely frightened for a little while. She circled the van waiting for an idea to hit. *"That's what I get for being a smart ass,"* she thought grimly. She thought about what Lola would have to say about her predicament, and it made her laugh out loud for just a moment until the seriousness of her state set in again.

She sat down on a rock, closed her eyes, and tried to empty her mind so she could stay calm and figure out the problem. Then she did something she had never done before. She asked for a vision to help her. She immediately got a picture of a streak of lightening coming out of the sky and hitting the top of the van. She opened her eyes and puzzled over what she had seen. She knew it meant something, but didn't know what. Then, she noticed a long, broken stick nearby which had fallen from one of the nearby trees. It was bent and crooked and she realized that it was shaped just like a streak of lightening, like in the vision. She remembered the open skylight on the top of the van and realized what she was supposed to do. Rather clumsily, Dawn climbed up on top of the car, carrying the stick, and used it to reach inside the skylight to the console and push the Door-Unlock button. It worked like a charm. She jumped in the van and drove to a small motel for the night. When she went out to dinner, she ordered a glass of wine and toasted to Spirit, to resourcefulness, and to the gifts of vision that had saved her.

From Dawn's Journal

What a scary thing that was! And so dangerous! It could have so easily gone wrong today. But here's the good news. I learned was to rely on my intuition and resourceful, and not be afraid to call in help from the divine. That vision saved me today—that's all there is to it.

Also, I learned that if you can see the humor in a situation, you're not likely to panic, run in circles, and die in the desert. I am so grateful for that!

CHAPTER 19

Vipassana Buddhist Retreat

The next morning, Dawn drove the van to an area in the desert outside of the town of Joshua Tree and began looking for the Vipassana Buddhist Retreat where she had arranged to spend a couple of nights. The sand-colored land around her was completely flat as far as she could see. Buildings hugged the earth in order to keep cool and were hard to see because they blended into the earth colors. Dawn was having a lot of trouble finding the place, but finally hit upon a bunch of low buildings and a sign made up of fallen trees in the shape of an old arbor that stretched across a dirt road. The sign said *Vipassana*. She drove up to the buildings, and when she got out of the car, four mongrel dogs rushed out of nowhere and surrounded her, barking and growling. An old woman rushed out of a tiny house and shooed the dogs away. She looked at Dawn up and down and said, "You're lucky these were my dogs. If they had been the wild dogs that live out here, they would have torn you apart." Then she went right back inside before Dawn could ask her anything.

Dawn wasn't sure of what to do at that point, so she approached a bigger building nearby with double screen doors. She knocked and got no answer. She tried again and then just walked in, calling as she went. A woman about Dawn's age appeared around the corner and greeted her. Her name was Laura, and she welcomed Dawn and offered her some tea. They sat in a large dining room with several tables and a small, adjoining sitting area. Laura explained that the old woman from the tiny house was a revered Buddhist leader, Arlene

Peterson, who owned the retreat compound. The compound consisted of the building they were in which held the dining area and kitchen. Then there was a retreat house, a large meditation plaza, and Arlene's tiny house. There was also an outdoor shower tent. The retreat house held five large bedrooms for retreat attendees and a small temple out back.

Laura had a great sense of humor and seemed genuinely glad for Dawn's company. She was originally from Rhode Island and had been working as a cook at the retreat for three months. She needed to finish preparing a meal, so Dawn offered to help her so they could continue talking. Dawn set the table while Laura cooked.

Laura explained that Arlene seldom made appearances. They might see her at mealtimes occasionally and at morning meditation which was held at seven o'clock every morning in the temple. Dawn would be expected to attend that early meditation. She also told Dawn that she could sleep in a small vacant house that was located down the road and belonged to the retreat center. Dianne would drive there in a little while and Dawn could follow in her car and get settled in.

After the simple, delicious vegetarian meal, Dawn followed in her van as Laura drove to the vacant house down a long dusty, dirt road. The house was just one big room with a small bedroom attached. Unfortunately, there was no bathroom. However, there was a sink inside and an outhouse in the backyard. Laura had work to do, so she showed Dawn around then left and told her to come back to the kitchen at dinnertime.

Looking out the windows, Dawn could see no other houses around, just flat sand, rocks, and scrub desert. She was quite alone, yet for some reason, she began to feel a bit uneasy, as if she were being watched. The fact was, she had felt a little uneasy the moment she first saw this little house, but couldn't quite put her finger on what it was that was bothering her. To ease her mind, she found an old radio and played it loudly, singing along while she looked around. She got out a book and read it in a dusty, but comfy old chair in the big room, just killing time. After a couple of hours, she took a break and headed to the back yard for the outhouse.

On the door of the little building was a small mask about as big as a fist, hanging by a nail. Dawn took one look at it, and her heart froze. The mask was painted black, white, and red and had an extraordinarily evil feel to it. Dawn knew that anyone would have felt the weird vibes emanating from the object, not just someone who was becoming sensitive to energy, as she was. Why someone had hung it on the door to the outhouse was a mystery and, as Dawn thought, *"a little mean."* After all, it was the only bathroom around for a mile.

There was no way that she was going to open the door to that outhouse, let alone go inside. She actually slowly backed away, keeping her eyes on it till she turned a corner and it was out of sight.

She ended up squatting behind a cactus in the yard to use the bathroom, hiding senselessly since there was no one around as far as she could see. She stayed inside and away from the outhouse for the rest of the day. She couldn't imagine what she would do if she had to use it in the middle of the night. It was out of the question.

In the evening, she headed back to the main retreat center. She showered in the shower tent and then went in to talk to Laura again. Dawn was in a cheerful mood, and they talked about their backgrounds some more. Dawn didn't mention the mask. She didn't know Laura and wasn't sure if the other woman would think she was crazy, although she felt absolutely correct in her readings about it.

At dinner, Arlene came in to dine with the two women. They spoke little while they ate, but Arlene did tell Dawn that she had been leading Buddhist retreats in this retreat center for twenty years. The first words that came to Dawn's mind in describing Arlene were "tough old bird." She had iron grey hair, a plump, round body draped in scarves of blue and green, and eyes that flashed intelligence and impatience. Dawn knew that she was reading her constantly during their meal.

After dinner, Arlene took Dawn aside and began to teach, which was unexpected, but a welcome surprise. She actually spoke for a couple of hours, almost non-stop, never pausing for any questions. She told Dawn about the importance of meditation, that it was the tried and true way to enlightenment. She also spoke of the circles of power, of women's power, of the power of nature. Dawn decided that Arlene felt like a Native American Shaman Buddhist. She was unique, to be sure. She seemed so close to God and nature, it just fit. Abruptly, the lecture ended and Arlene left. Laura, who had been in the kitchen all that time, came out and told Dawn it was time to lock up and for Dawn to go back to the vacant house, and that she would see her at meditation in the morning.

Dawn got in the van and drove slowly in the pitch dark with her high beams on back to the house. She found it with a little trouble and sat looking at the house in the moonlight. Then she got out a flashlight from the back of the van and brought her sleeping bag in through the front door. As she put the bag on top of the bed, she was suddenly seized with such a deep, cold sense of danger and fear, it stopped her cold. She looked around the room and out of the windows into the black ink of night. She didn't see anything or hear anything except absolute quiet, but she knew with certainty that she was in danger. She flew into action. Grabbing up her sleeping bag, she flew back to the van and locked the doors. She started the van and drove in the dark back towards the retreat center. She just needed to get out of there and away from that house. As she drove, to her horror, she could hear growling noises following close to the car. Something hit the driver's side of the van numerous times as she drove over the axle-breaking dirt road. The hairs on her arms stood on end the whole trip back, and she found herself yelling out loud in terror. Whatever it was, it was dangerous. Dawn prayed that she would not have to find out what it was. As she neared the main building, the noises and growling stopped. Dawn parked right next to the front screen door of the kitchen building, which had a big porch light, and turned off the ignition. She didn't dare get out of the car. After a while, she climbed into the back of the van and huddled down in her sleeping bag, keeping the flashlight right next to her. She lay awake most of the night listening, but didn't hear anything more. Finally she fell asleep until sunrise, awakening stiff and cold.

She poked her head up and looked around outside of the van. It looked peaceful. All was quiet. Had she imagined the craziness the night before? *"No freaking way did I imagine that!"* she thought. Yet, it didn't seem real in the light of day. She opened the doors and let the cold desert air inside the van. It was getting close to the time of meditation, so she went and washed a little at the sink in the shower tent and changed her shirt. Afterwards she walked to the temple and found no one there yet, so she waited in a small courtyard, sitting on a bench that was warming in the sun.

The desert was uncannily still. Dawn could hear nothing, not even the few humans inside the nearby buildings. She found herself falling into a meditation of sorts in the quiet. And then, magic happened. Quick as the blink of an eye, the courtyard was suddenly filled with jackrabbits—huge rabbits with their large ears standing above their heads like antennae. A half dozen or so of them hopped close to Dawn into the courtyard and froze, listening, sniffing. Dawn was awestruck and didn't move a muscle. The hush in the yard was suspended as human and rabbits regarded each other. And then in a flash they were gone, hopping off in all directions. Dawn was stunned with wonder. She knew she had just witnessed a gift. She smiled a huge smile and was filled with a warm thankfulness.

Later, she looked up what jackrabbits meant spiritually in a book in Arlene's library. They are a symbol of being a visionary and planning your future with imagination and wisdom. Dawn took that definition as encouragement that her quest was on track.

After some time, Arlene and Laura arrived for meditation. The temple was a beautiful, low-lying building with many windows, flying prayer flags and colorful pillows on the floor. The three women chose pillows, and Arlene gave Dawn some basic instructions. She told her to follow her breath, in and out, and try to clear her thoughts. She said that when Dawn found her mind wandering to the past or the future, that she should call it back to the present, the stillness, and her breath because the mind had to be trained to this type of practice. She also said that every time she called her mind back, she could consider it a victory and that she should be gentle with herself and not frustrated. She said, "We are all here practicing."

They sat in meditation together, listening to the morning desert awaken and the extraordinary quiet. They remained for about an hour, and it was one of the most profound things Dawn had ever experienced. She knew that many people could sit for hours, but she had not built up that kind of stamina yet. An hour was a long time for her, but with this teacher, the stillness was contagious and powerful, and the time flew.

Over breakfast of oatmeal and yogurt, Dawn told Laura about what had happened to her the night before. Laura couldn't explain it, except to suggest that maybe the wild dogs had scared her. Dawn nodded but didn't quite accept that explanation. Do wild dogs throw themselves at a moving car? What about the overpowering sensation of being watched? What about the mask, the sensation of evil? She didn't know, but it sure hadn't felt like dogs. She guessed that she might never know, but she was glad she had trusted her sensitivities and got the heck out of there.

Laura suggested that Dawn sleep in the Retreat House that night and asked if she felt like helping out a bit. She told her that the retreat house needed vacuuming because it hadn't really been cleaned after their recent retreat. Dawn told her she would be happy to do it. She felt like she needed to do something. Everyone else was so busy, and besides, she really wanted to see inside the big retreat house.

So, after the meal, she gathered up cleaning supplies and headed over to start cleaning. The Retreat House consisted of five bedrooms and three bathrooms plus a meeting room. There were spiritual objects such as statues of holy teachers, many of whom Dawn didn't recognize, and gongs, spiritual pictures, and symbols in every room. There was a tall table holding a huge silver punch bowl at the front door. She couldn't even guess the purpose of that. As she cleaned, she very quickly realized that the house had little visitors. Mice. In fact, the more she cleaned, the more evidence of desert mice she found, and she started to get creeped out. There were mouse droppings everywhere. Then she found a couple of mice lying dead in closets from being poisoned. Her skin started to crawl, and she found herself jumping at shadows. The word Hantavirus kept coming to mind like a new mantra.

She continued to vacuum and clean, and then sterilized the sink and counters as best she could. However, by the time she was done, she was grossed out and wouldn't dream of sleeping in the house that night. Sleep would never come in a place where she knew there was a chance of mice running over her in the dark. Just, nope.

As she finished the front entrance hall, her last room, she opened the front door, and a huge white scorpion darted inside. She had never seen such a thing. She wondered if it was an albino or a species she had just never heard of. Either way, she yelped and jumped out of the way. Then she looked around for something to catch it with. She couldn't very well just let it loose in the house, yet the scorpion was so big, she didn't know what to do. It was like trying to catch a small rat that scurried and threatened to sting a body, and it was fast too. Finally, she picked up the heavy silver punch bowl and plunked it down, inverted, on top of the scorpion. She thought, "*Oh God! I know I need to get rid of this little guy, but I'm probably using some sacred ritual bowl here.*" Looking in some dresser drawers, she found some poster board and slipped it underneath the bowl. She barely managed to pick up the scorpion with the heavy bowl and threw the creature out the front door and back into the desert. As she watched it scurry away, she suddenly felt that she had been sent some sort of visitation. Of course, she didn't know what it meant, but felt that it was a warning and a blessing at the same time.

Later, she asked Laura about the meaning of Scorpion, and they looked it up in Arlene's book. It said that the Scorpion represented protection, and when the Scorpion makes an appearance in our lives, it is beckoning us to consider how we feel about the controls in our life. They can also represent rebirth and new beginnings.

Dawn knew that she had always resented people trying to control her life. At this point, she wanted to take back the control of her own life. It was one of the reasons she had felt compelled to make this trip. She wanted to place control in the hands of Spirit to guide her to where she was supposed to be. That night, she prayed about that before going to bed. Of course, she also realized that she was a Scorpio. Maybe she was just being greeted by a little brother. Dawn kind of liked that idea.

Dawn slept in the van again that night, free from mice, scorpions, wild dogs, and who knows what else. The night was uneventful, and in the morning, she bid goodbye to Laura. She didn't see Arlene again, as she never appeared out of her little house that morning. So, she pulled out into the dirt road and left Joshua Tree behind her, heading to the Palm Springs airport and home to Louisiana.

From Dawn's Journal

I've been thinking about the evil-feeling mask on the outhouse. I think that some people might jump to conclusions and think something about demons or some such. But now that I've had a minute to think about it, I think it was just a warning to me to be careful on this trip. Lynn had warned me that I might run across people who might try to take advantage of my "searching" state of mind. That is what my intuition is telling me now, so I will double up on my carefulness. I don't think there were demons in the desert chasing my car. But just ask me if I am willing to go out there again at night and have a look around, and I will laugh you off the planet! It was scary, but I'm going with Lynn's warning anyway.

I was also thinking about meditation and enlightenment. Arlene said you can reach enlightenment after years of meditation, and I'm sure she's right. But I've heard from other sources that it can be achieved in this age in the blink of an eye. I sure like that idea, of course. It's all about believing that it can be done. But how do I make myself believe that? Perhaps if I start by training myself daily to believe positive things and talking to myself in a positive voice, I can get closer.

<h1 style="text-align:center">CHAPTER 20</h1>

From Dawn's Journal

I'm at the Palm Springs airport now, coming to the end of my California portion of my spiritual journey, with some time to kill. So I did some googling about visions and ran across an article about the different types of psychic visions. The article said that not all psychics get prophetic visions of disaster. Thank God I never did. I have received helpful messages, yes, but scary premonitions of plane crashes and war, no. I couldn't imagine living with that. That's the sort of thing that makes for what they call "good TV". Now that's a scary concept.

The author of the article said that there was a difference between true visions, fear, and visions that the ego conjures up, and that there was a way to tell the difference. A psychic could check for certain criteria. If the vision was a quick flash or a picture that came out of nowhere with no emotion attached to it, then that was a true vision. She said that a quick vision needed to be noticed and heeded because, as the author's teacher had told her many times, "Always pay attention when spirits speak because they don't repeat themselves."

The author went on to say if the vision was born of fear, it may not be a true one. It might be only a reflection of the psychic's or the client's fears. A psychic could tell a fear vision because he/she will feel fear it in the stomach, and the fear sometimes intensifies and creates horrific visions.

Finally, she said that if the ego created the vision, the psychic's mind will be racing with thoughts and emotions, and the vision may go on and on. The ego likes to bedazzle people, and so this is not a true vision but one born of the psychic's own heroics.

I didn't entirely agree with the article. I agree that my quick flash visions are reliable and strong. And I agree that there is usually no emotion attached to my visions—sometimes, but not usually. But I'm not sure that I agree that a true vision is always quick. I have had movie-type visions that developed slowly. There were no emotions attached to the movies for me, but they do sometimes drag on, and they often proved to be accurate. So, if these things can be labeled and differentiated, and I suspect deeply that they can't be, then the article was hit-and-miss for me. But I found it very interesting that she had given the subject that much thought and consideration. At least the author was trying. I was delighted to have found something to read that covered what I was experiencing.

As for my visions, I believe that I'm some sort of conduit. Visions just pass through me to deliver information. Not very flattering actually, like I'm just some bit of fiber optics carrying a phone message. Sometimes I don't even know what the messages mean, but I've learned to take them all seriously.

CHAPTER 21

"Get this, Lola. I actually climbed up on top of the van, reached down with a stick through the skylight, and pushed the door-open button," said Dawn into the phone, as she sat waiting for her flight to board in Palm Springs. "Can you believe it?"

She was met with quiet on the other end of the phone. "Lola, are you there?"

"Are you telling me you climbed up on top of the van?"

"I did! I'm sure I must have looked like an ox doing the cha-cha, but I got up there. What else could I do? There was nobody else around."

"Well, that's it, Dawn. You've been looking for a miracle in your life, and that was it. It was a miracle you got up there. Man, I would have killed to have seen that. I'm actually impressed."

Dawn laughed. "I'm kinda impressed with me too! God only knows how I didn't kill myself. But that was nothing. Wait till I tell you about the Vipassana Buddhist retreat and Arlene Peterson."

Dawn went on to describe the Buddhist compound, the peaceful hours of meditation, and the teachings from Arlene. "Meditating for that long was so hard at first, but I grew to love it after a while. My brain is usually going a mile a minute…"

"Your mouth too," said Lola, giggling.

"That too," chuckled Dawn. "But meditation slows everything down. I felt actually peaceful instead of my usual anxious, obnoxious self. We are so doing this when I get back."

"I'll put it on the list," smiled Lola.

"OK, got to run now—they are starting to board. I'm coming home, Lola. Get ready!"

CHAPTER 22

"If I didn't believe you before, Dawn, I sure do now!" said Judith. The five Sistahs sat in front of the Gumbeaux Sistahs Gallery. They had to squeeze in to fit, but they all wanted to sit on the bench there while looking up at the spectacular show developing right in front of their eyes.

The telephone wires running right over their heads were covered with cawing, black, iridescent crows. And more joined the noisy group every minute.

"I've never seen anything like it!" said Bea, her mouth open as she looked up at all the corvids.

"What do you suppose it means?" asked Helen. "There seems to be some sort of message here, don't you think? An urgent one by the looks of things. When we looked it up before it said that it meant that God was calling you. But you went on that journey already. So, now what?"

"Not only that," said Lola, "but while you were gone, they weren't out here raising all this racket. And I watered your yard while you were gone, and there were none hanging around there either. They were apparently waiting for you, my friend,"

Dawn was quiet for a minute while contemplating the overhead murder.

"I think you're right, Helen. And, yes, I think it is urgent."

"Well, do you have any idea what it is?"

"This is as near as I can figure, Helen. There has been so much happening to me since the crows first showed up. And it's all part of this same spiritual journey. I'm learning so much, and I have to say, it's making me happy. It even makes me feel closer to all y'all, if that's even possible!" she said, laughing.

"You do seem happier, Dawn. You're actually glowing these days," said Helen nodding with approval.

"She's probably radioactive," smirked Lola, and Dawn nudged her hard with her elbow.

"Hey! Assault is not very spiritual!" laughed Lola.

"Don't get sidetracked, dear," Bea told Dawn. "Tell us what you were trying to say. And Lola, zip it."

Lola faked a pout then looked at Dawn expectantly, wanting her to continue.

"Like I was saying, this journey I'm on is making a huge difference in my life. I think the crows are telling me that it's just getting started. That I need to keep going. I keep getting that I'm supposed to help others on their spiritual journeys too."

"Ooh, I think you're onto something, my friend. I'm getting goosie-bumps," said Helen with a shiver.

"Me too," said Judith. "How would you go about doing that, Dawn?"

"That's the big question, isn't it?" said Dawn. "I'm not sure where to start."

"Hmmm, can I make a suggestion?" asked Bea.

"Please do, Bea. I need help!"

"Why don't you make a list? You could put down points of what you've learned so far and add to them as you go along."

"Can I make a suggestion?" asked Lola with a smirk.

"No, you can't, dear. Unless it's serious," said Bea, giving Lola a stern eye.

Lola sank back in her seat. "Oh, y'all are no fun sometimes."

Dawn spoke up, "How about this, sistahs? I can keep the list in my journal. I have my next appointment with Lynn tomorrow. Can we meet again afterwards to talk about this list? It helps me to run things past you."

"Sounds good," said Judith. "And Dawn, I think what you are doing is important."

"Hopefully, it will help people. I feel a little like a fake because I don't know what I'm doing, but I'm sincere in my desire to help." She looked up and added, "And maybe once we start this list, the crows will back off."

Lola stood up suddenly. "You know, one thing I think those crows mean is that if you sit underneath them long enough, you will get pooped on! I have that feeling we're about to learn that one the hard way!"

The Sistahs jumped to their feet and scrambled towards the gallery entrance.

CHAPTER 23

That night, Dawn sat in front of her computer with a glass of wine, composing an email to the Sistahs. She sat back to read what she'd written.

Dear Sistahs,

Here's what I have so far on the list:
How to Start a Spiritual Journey

1. Beware of crow poop!

She chuckled out loud and hit send.

CHAPTER 24

Dawn reached into her car and pulled out a piece of paper that she'd printed from her computer. She handed it to Lola, saying, "I just wanted to show you this. I got another email from Lynn last week while she was out of town. I didn't check my email very much while I was traveling, so I came home to this. It's starting to get awkward, Lola. Take a look."

Lola took the email and read:

Dear Dan:

I'm in Sedona! It's all so changed, and yet the essence remains the same. Just fantastic!

I had a reading with a woman named Sondraya first thing. My new friend, Dawn, told me about her. She's so powerful! She just glows with energy and power. I'm jazzed and encouraged about life just being around her.

When I get back, maybe we can do coffee and catch up, old friend?

Lynn

"Oh boy," said Lola, rolling her eyes. "She wants to meet Dan for coffee? You're in trouble now."

"Well, that can't happen, obviously," said Dawn.

"Won't she think it's weird that her good 'old friend' won't ever meet her in person? She's only right across the lake from us."

"She might," said Dawn, shaking her head. "But what can I do? Not only have I not figured out her relationship with Dan yet, but she and I are starting to be, as she said, kind of—friends. I would hate to mess it all up. It's a very confusing position to be in."

Lola looked at her friend, shaking her head. "Just know that the time for honesty is coming. At least you have an excuse for not meeting her right away. You leave for Sedona at the end of the week yourself."

Dawn perked up. "I can't wait, Lola. And you can best believe that I already made an appointment with Sondraya for another reading when I get there—first thing."

"Well, just remember me back home. I'll be waiting to hear every word she says."

◆◆◆◆◆

That night Dawn sat in front of her computer with her second glass of courage in the form of three year old Merlot and wrote another email to Lynn, trying to be as vague and evasive as possible.

Dear Lynn:

Just a quick note here, but I would love to hear more about your trip to Sedona and your meeting with Sondraya.

Meanwhile, I'm getting ready to go out of town myself, and I'll be gone a couple of weeks. I'll check in with you when I get back.

Sincerely,
Dan

CHAPTER 25

Dawn met one more time with Lynn before she left on her trip. Lynn had just returned from Sedona and was in a jovial mood. She chattered and talked so excitedly and fast that she sounded like a typewriter. Doling out her homemade pralines to Dawn, she explained, "My mom always made these for special occasions: Christmas, graduations, Mardi Gras, springing my brother out of prison…"

Dawn laughed at first then looked at her friend to see if she was serious. Lynn just winked at her and went on, "But I make them all the time. We should always be celebrating, right?"

They sat at the small table embellished with crystals and tarot card decks where they had held their first appointment. "I love the furniture in your place, Lynn. You have some very interesting pieces. They look like they all have a story behind each of them."

Lynn chuckled and said, "You want to hear a story about my latest piece? A friend gave me a sleigh bed, and I had to call over a handyman to come and help me set it up. The bed wiggled and squeaked like crazy, so he said, "You don't want that bed to be squeaking like that." I looked at him and said, "Just what do you think I'm going to be doing in it?" She laughed uproariously.

"Oh God, kid. You should have seen this face. He was so embarrassed. When you get to be this age you can say almost anything. It's so damn much fun. Well, you're a lot like that yourself."

Dawn could just imagine how that meeting had gone. She felt a little sorry for the handyman running into the force that was Lynn

Lamoree, but she had to agree about getting away with saying things as you got older. It was fun. The Sistahs did it all the time.

Then Lynn became serious and said, "I want to tell you something, Dawn, and I hope you'll remember this. You are to be a professional in your desire to help other people. You have the gift of being a psychic. Don't be shy or embarrassed or act like you don't know something. You do. People will always be seeking more knowledge about their lives. And I can tell that you feel like you need to be an expert before you get started. You're thinking, 'If I don't know everything, then how do I start?' But I can tell you that in this business, if you have the gift, which you do, how you get started is—you just start."

Dawn protested, "But I'm not sure I want to be a professional, Lynn. I think I'm just supposed to help people with this gift, if that's what it is. And I'm even unsure about that. But the idea of practicing it on other people is terrifying. I'm going to make a total ass of myself, and what if I'm wrong?"

Lynn shook her head. "No you're not going to make an ass out of yourself. OK, let me put it to you this way; you can't save your ass and your face at the same time! Ooh, that's good. I'll have to remember that one. Oh Kid, I'm full of them."

She went on, "Listen, I've always been clairvoyant and clairaudient. Sometimes it's not a gift. When I was a kid, I lived about eleven blocks from my school, and I walked home. When I got to my street, I would know right at that point if my mother was drunk or not. I could see her being sloppy in my mind. I would then walk eight more houses and put my foot on my lawn and at that point, I would know if it was dangerous for me or not. No matter what, I had to go into the house anyway. It didn't matter what I knew. I was just a kid and I was trained to be obedient. Psychic ability is not always a gift. I didn't consider *that* a gift."

"And sometimes it still gets me in trouble. I was up at the clubhouse the other day, and I suddenly felt this woman looking at me. I looked back at her, and I could read her like a book. I could feel that she didn't approve of something about me. I took one step toward her and looked her right in the eye and I said, "Lay off." Lynn started to chuckle.

Dawn eyes opened wide and she shook her head and replied, "Oh boy. What did she do?"

"She looked at me and said, 'You think you can read my mind?'"

"And I said, 'I don't think I can read your mind. I can. And I don't like what I'm hearing. That's not alright with me. Take it somewhere else!' It just popped right out of me. I don't normally talk like that. Well, maybe I do." She laughed with delight.

Dawn stared at the other woman. She still didn't know what to make of her sometimes, so she impulsively blurted out, "Lynn, you're so crazy!"

Lynn replied with a twinkle, "Yes, I'm all that and more. But, listen, Dawn, here's a tip for you about clients. It's important not to get carried away with trying to make a client feel good. They may not be glad at all at what you have to tell them. They may even get up and leave or they might say, 'Well, I didn't expect you to tell me that! You didn't tell me anything positive or wonderful. And now I've already paid you the money and I have to leave.' And I tell them, 'Well, yes, you do.'" She laughed loudly and went on, "And if they don't ever want to come back, that's OK too. I tell them to go find somebody who will bullshit them. If they want to call me and make another appointment, we'll see if I have time to see them. Could I use the money? Well sure, but I will not kiss anybody's ass. No way, honey baby. I'm going to tell them the truth no matter what because that is my job. And now it will be yours too."

"And listen," Lynn went on. "I also want to talk to you about religion, Dawn. Many religions will tell you that you're 'edging God out' with your practice. I mean, what do they mean 'edging God out'? What have I ever done to edge God out?"

Dawn said seriously, "I don't think God is ever edged out."

"Well, I don't either. And where do they think I got this gift from anyway? But my point is that there are a lot of neurotic beliefs out there that people expect you to go along with."

Lynn continued, "And of course, in our line of work, we have the 'WooWoo's.' That's what some people call us. I am a minister and can marry people. The name on my minister license actually says 'Lynn WooWoo Lamoree,' if you can believe that. I thought it was funny."

Dawn found that she could believe it easily.

Lynn laughed heartily and went on, "But, unfortunately, some WooWoo's have this need to make themselves look better than anybody else because they feel competitive and their egos got away from them. They want to appear to be more informed or better acquainted about psychic phenomena, and sometimes they even do this by scaring the hell out of people and reading about the dark side. And that's just wrong. Although I have to admit, just for fun, when I teach an Astrology or Tarot class, I always begin with the words, 'You're going to die…in a foreign country…in the gutter… with a sword in your throat!' Then I step back and say, 'And if you believe that, you can leave now because I don't teach that, and I don't want you to carry that out of this room.' Because it is not true. Astrology and Tarot have been used at times to create fear. And we've all seen how fear can move people to following some untrue path like lemmings right off the cliff with no independent thinking at all. Fear is a dangerous thing. And it's wrong. Tarot is filled with love. Nothing but love.

"So, don't try to be mysterious or dark for entertainment purposes, not that I think you would, but I'm just saying. I don't go there. I am clairvoyant, and I hear and know things that I know to be true for me. Therefore, I repeat it to my clients. It's not because I read it in a book or memorized something, but because it was in my brain or my heart already. That's how I work. And that's what you have. You have the same ability, so you can penetrate deeply with your intuition and your visions.

"Now, let me ask you, when I pull your astrological chart, does that chart make you do anything? No. It provides you with something like a blueprint of what your 'House' is going to look like and what kind of tools you have to work with. Here's an example: let's say that you did the birth chart of a king, and then you did one of a person who lived on the streets—but he was the king of the street people. The king of the streets looked after his charges and saw to it that when a new guy came in to the area, there was a place for him. He found out where everyone could go to get something to eat and where the best dumpsters were. He was 'king' of the homeless. And so some of the exact same charts will come up for both the royal king and the homeless king. But those charts wouldn't make either king do anything. It just reads their lives as they are. It is a tool only, but a powerful one. It lets me know quite a bit."

Lynn continued, "Now about your trip to Sedona. You're going right?"

Dawn nodded.

"You need to address Sedona as a fabulous opportunity to run and play, and a place to plant a lot of seeds. You just went through this past year of letting go of a lot of stuff. It's been, what I call, a Surrender Year. And now that's over. Now you are back at the beginning of a cycle instead of the end. You're already feeling a desire to start planting seeds, and by that I mean, of course, change, renewal, new beginnings, increased self-confidence, and courage — and you have a lot of courage, by the way. There are so many new decisions coming your way.

"OK, so all this will give you a basis for some things that I would encourage you to think about. You don't have to. You can walk out of here and say, 'OK, I listened, and that's enough of that.' Or you can approach it and see if there is any truth in it for you. The essence of where you are right now is seeking truth. And it's natural for you to want to know everything, from several points of view. I've said this to you before—you have this tremendous desire to be a walking encyclopedia. This comes from a real desire to be in control."

Dawn nodded, "There's some truth in that. That's how I ran my business back home."

Lynn went on, "You like to hold the power, but that's diminishing now. Your ego is softening. You used to think 'Why don't they do what I want? I mean, I'm reasonable!'"

Dawn laughed out loud. "Yes, that sounds like me."

"Good, you can see the humor in that now. How do I know that about you? Because I have some of those same qualities in me, and I recognize it. But the more you can let other people have their own power, the better off you will be. Because, as you are moving through the second half of life now, it would be a good idea to let things turn inward so that they serve you. Claim power over yourself. Over your emotions. And then you will be in charge of your life, not everybody else's. Now that's true power."

Dawn asked, "Lynn, how do you know who you truly are?"

"Because it pours out of me. I can't help it or stop it. I listen to my heart. I started studying Tarot and Astrology many years ago. Back then, I went to teachers, and I listened and saluted to what they said. But I've thrown out three-quarters of what I was taught because now I know my truth and not something that somebody told me I had to believe. You will do that too."

Lynn then had Dawn choose three tarot cards. She studied them, and said, "OK, here's something. You have a fabulous business mind. You always need to be in business for yourself, but you knew that already. But it will be a different business this time, and you will have a good time figuring out what it will be. Enjoy your ambition, it is part of your creativity."

She squinted and then suddenly looked up, and asked, "Ok, Dawn, wait, do you have urinary problems? "

Surprised, Dawn said, "What? Uh, I don't think so. Why?

"I see that you need to drink more water. Now, did I say eight glasses a day? No. Many medical sites online say that we need eight glasses a day. Somebody got a hold of that notion and kept saying it out loud, over and over again, until everyone accepted it as gospel. More lemmings at work! You'll know how much your body needs. Just pay attention to it."

She blinked and looked at Dawn seriously. "So when are you going to Sedona?"

"Very soon," answered Dawn.

"Good," nodded Lynn. "You have work to do. And now, it's time to go." She rose to her feet and started walking to the front door. "Call when you're there, and let's get together when you get back. And have a wonderful time, Dawn."

— ◆◆◆ —

As before, Dawn walked out of Lynn's house a little stunned. She now knew a lot more about the other woman, and, as crazy as she seemed, Dawn found her delightful. This was troubling since, firstly, Lynn was looney, and secondly, she may have once been her husband's lover. With that thought, she stamped her foot on the sidewalk, as she realized with a horrible shock, *"Dammit. With all that was going on, I got distracted again. Lynn talks so fast and has a lot to say. I got carried away with listening to her, and I still don't know about her and Dan!"*

CHAPTER 26

Welcome to Sedona – the Light Center

Dawn flew into Flagstaff, Arizona, rented another car—not a van this time. She drove to Sedona from the north, winding down a very windy road, dropping a thousand feet in altitude into Oak Creek Canyon. She shot past miles of trees, rocks, and woods, and the world suddenly opened up into one of the most amazing views in the world. Huge, red rocks towered everywhere she looked; the flame color ignited by the sun. It was breathtaking.

She lost her mind for a moment in all that beauty. The road was one lane with steep drop-offs, but she actually let go of the wheel of the car for a second, grabbed her phone and starting taking pictures of the most beautiful place she'd ever seen. Occasionally she would nudge the wheel with a hand or an elbow. She came to her senses in a minute and got back to careful driving. She thought, *"I'll have to remember that if I drive this road again. I'll watch out for crazy tourists with no hands on the wheel!"*

Travel Magazine and others have called Sedona the "Most Beautiful Place in America." Dawn just wanted to call it heaven.

She had once heard a story about Sedona, but was not sure if it was true. Supposedly, the land is so enchanted that the local Native Americans would not make their homes there. They only visited when they wished to make special ceremonies to the Great Spirit. Dawn thought that if the Great Spirit lived anywhere for its beauty, it would be Sedona.

She reached town and drove around taking in the otherworldly views of the red mountains before heading to her destination, The Light Center in Sedona.

She found it up in the hills above the eastern part of town. The Light Center consisted of several buildings, the main one being a large geodesic dome with beautiful gardens, stained glass doors, and a million-dollar view of the red mountains. She parked and entered the main building, noting a wooden bench just inside for leaving shoes. She pulled off her sandals and looked around, but she didn't see anyone. The place was dead quiet, and she wasn't sure what to do. She called out and waited, but no one answered, so she ventured further into the building. There were several closed doors off a long hall on the first floor, none of which said "office" or anything like that, so none invited her knock. She had to admire the large canvases covering every wall with colorful, metaphysical-themed art. They were fascinating, and she would take pictures of them later to send to the Sistahs. At the end of the hall, she found a winding iron staircase which she took, calling out as she ascended. She found herself in a large, circular room surrounded by huge windows and a view of Sedona to die for. There she found Paul, the owner of the Center, sitting at a table in a corner doing some paperwork.

Paul was about fifty, bald, portly and wore all white clothes. Dawn walked up quietly and introduced herself, telling him that she had a reservation at the Center. He asked her to sit down and then just stared at her for a minute or two before he talked. For someone who looked like some sort of shaman, he talked like a New York businessman, clipped and to the point. He told Dawn about the Center and how it came into existence. He said that he had come to Sedona years before and had looked around for a place to build. He bought the property and was trying to decide where to situate the main building when a boulder rolled down the mountain towards him and stopped cold at his feet. He took that as a sign and built the Center on that very spot. He said that people from all over the world come to the Center to stay. He mentioned that his girlfriend, Maya, lived in the smaller geodesic dome house behind the main building. There were two private bedrooms downstairs for rent and a group sleeping quarters upstairs where Dawn would stay. Lynn always stayed in the group accommodations and had recommended them to Dawn so that she would be sure to meet some interesting people.

Paul then basically dismissed Dawn and went back to his work. So Dawn went back to her car and got her overnight case. She hauled it upstairs to the group room and went about arranging her belongings. She found a pillow and mat to sleep on in a cabinet and put her grip next to it. Then she went back out to look at the town and find a meal.

When she returned in the evening, she met Naomi, a woman who stayed at the Center on a semi-permanent work-exchange basis. Naomi was about fifty, thin to the bone with blonde hair, a few missing teeth, wrinkled skin, and a heart of pure gold. She and Dawn got along very well. She told Dawn that she had been living with her boyfriend in Sedona, but that he turned out to be a pretty bad guy and kicked her out. She also shared with Dawn that he used to pull her cheeks to the side when they made love so that her wrinkles would smooth out. Their conversation left Dawn thinking, "*What a sweetheart. I hope he comes to his senses and finds himself—in a pit of rattlesnakes in the middle of the desert.*" Naomi had no place to go, so she came to the Light Center and traded her stay for work. She wasn't sure where she would end up next. Dawn was careful to treat Naomi like absolute gold. The woman had been through enough, and she deserved better.

There were a lot of overnight guests at the Center that evening. Dawn wandered around in the main room from one group to another, hearing their stories. There were three women who were dermatologists from back east staying there for a medical conference in town. There was a couple on a cross-country trip heading for Florida. Out on the deck, she met two men who were peering through a large brass telescope at the night sky. One of the men told her that he was from the Pleiades, a group of stars located in the constellation Orion's belt. The other man started laughing and then shook the Pleadian's hand and said, "That's great. I'm actually from Jupiter myself." Dawn was astounded to realize that they were both being serious. She was soon to discover that there were a lot of people from other planets living in Sedona. She honestly didn't know what to make of them, but she loved meeting them. They tended to have livelier conversations than your average Joe or Jane.

Apparently, people from all over and many walks of life stayed at the Center. Dawn wanted to meet them all.

Later that night, she spread out her bed roll and pillow in a corner of the big room, lay her sleeping bag on top of it and tried to sleep surrounded by several other people. It was difficult. The energy of all the people in one room kept her awake for hours. Finally, she drifted off.

She wasn't asleep long before she was awakened in the night by someone shaking her shoulder. She opened her eyes and looked up to see a man who she was sure had to be a Greek god holding her hand and talking to her. He was one of the most beautiful men she had ever seen. Still, her head was full of sleep. She thought dreamily, *"Is he asking me to fly away to Olympus with him? Or maybe offering me immortality along with a cool goddess name—Akirren of the Lone Oak Woods—something like that? Lord, I hope so."* She dreamily smiled at the thought. Suddenly, her head cleared, and she realized the man hovering above her was real. She was able to make out what he was saying. It had nothing to do with Olympus. He was asking where he could find a sleeping roll and pillow. Dawn laughed at herself, but smoothed down her hair too, just in case. Then she pointed the bedroll cabinet out to him, and he thanked her and said he would see her in the morning. She went back to sleep with a big smile on her face and looked forward to daylight.

In the morning, she found out that the Greek god's name was Erich, and he was from Maui and visiting his son in Sedona. He ran a center in Hana similar to the Light Center and told Dawn simply that he lived in paradise. She believed him. Erich was very handsome and charming, and every woman in the Center sort of twittered within thirty feet of him. Dawn figured the man never lacked for female company in his life.

That morning, she hung around the Center and made friends with Erich and a woman named Krysta, who ran a real estate appraisal company in Tennessee. Dawn really liked Krysta, who was down to earth and had a great sense of humor. Dawn sat outside talking in the sun with Erich and Krysta for the better part of the morning, and they all made plans to go to the Sedona Arts Festival together that week.

While Dawn sat there with her new friends, a man and woman arrived at the center and offered a free healing session to anyone who wanted to participate, using a special breathing and healing technique. Dawn decided to try it. The session was held in the Center's meditation room, which was a round room with a mini altar containing several candles and pictures of spiritual leaders. Many colorful pillows were strewn around the room. Four other people attended the session. They made themselves comfortable on the pillows and were instructed to breathe in through their noses and out through their mouths with eyes relaxed and closed. The flow of breath was supposed to be non-stop, which was very uncomfortable to Dawn at first, but then she got the hang of it. Time passed and before she knew it, she began to see colorful visions. She saw archetypal and universal subjects and goddesses in the cosmos among twirling stars—that sort of thing. They were hypnotic and looked somehow like giant, Renaissance-style paintings. Then she found herself coming to her senses, as if she had passed out. But she felt wonderful. To her astonishment, two hours had passed in the session.

The session leaders explained that this was a "direct meditative technique to access the divine." Everyone went around the room sharing their experience. They were astonished when Dawn told them the images that she saw, which embarrassed her a little. She felt a bit dramatic. She had just assumed that everyone was experiencing those things, but most people said that they had simply been extremely relaxed and had a feeling of safety and happiness. It occurred to Dawn that perhaps her mind welcomed and embraced the chance to show her a cool vision. Something divine and very pleasant. It was the first time that she felt that she could call in a vision using her will. The first time that she felt a level of control over a vision. Later she would experiment with this control often and would find, to her astonishment, that she could ask for a vision and it would come. She felt that this would have a profound impact on her spiritual quest in the future and on the way she could help others too.

Later that afternoon, Dawn got in her car and headed out to the red rocks. She spent the rest of the day hiking in the desert. She brought a newly purchased tarot deck with her because she wanted the energy of the red mountains to bless the deck as she learned to use it.

Although she had brought a big plastic bottle of water with her, she ran out of it much quicker than she planned and began to feel dehydrated in the desert. Dawn knew how dangerous this can be, so she got back to the car as soon as she could. By the time she got there, she felt like some sort of desert animal exposed to the elements. But it felt good too. She felt like an athlete, strong, and healthy. Fortunately, she had loaded the car up with bottled water and she could drink her fill.

That night, she took herself out to celebrate arriving in Sedona, her good health, and the new vision experience with sushi and sake and then went back to fall asleep at the Center.

The following day, Dawn took a drive around Sedona and some neighboring towns to have a look around. She visited two Native American ruins sites: Tuzigoot, and Montezuma Castle. Both were National Monuments and Dawn found them breathtaking. She ended up spending the night in a nearby town and drove back to Sedona in the morning to meet up with Erich and Krysta. They planned to go to the Sedona Arts Festival that day. When she arrived, she found that her friends had already left, but had left a message for her to meet them there.

Dawn hurried over to the festival and found her two new friends along with the Light Center owner, Paul, and his girlfriend, Maya.

When Dawn walked up to the group, Paul, said, "Well, Dawn, it seems as if someone had themselves a great time last night!" He looked at her and winked.

She looked from Paul to a smiling Maya, confused, and asked, "What are we talking about here?"

"Oh, c'mon we heard you last night in the meditation room," said Paul grinning. "You were screaming and moaning—having a good old time. Who were you with anyway?"

Dawn stole a look at Erich and Krysta, who suddenly got very busy looking at their feet. They were busily ignoring Paul and were having a hard time not laughing.

Catching on, Dawn said, "Well, Paul. I do hope whoever it was had a terrific time, but unfortunately, it wasn't me. I was out of town last night."

Paul looked disappointed. Dawn had the distinct feeling that he had enjoyed the idea of her having a roll in his meditation room. Maya just shrugged.

Paul and Maya walked away to see some nearby booths, and Dawn turned to Erich and Krysta, smiling and said, "What have you two been up to? I can't leave you alone for a minute." They cracked up and then put their arms around me and each other. They had apparently been having a great time, in and out of the meditation room, and they were obviously crazy about each other. It was wonderful being around them. New love made them both very funny, and Dawn was happy for them.

The festival turned out to be very enjoyable. A musician named Estevan, who dressed like Zorro, played acoustic guitar beautifully while Dawn and friends strolled from one exhibit to another. Artists who displayed their crafts had to be juried into this show, so every exhibit was professional and interesting.

After a while, they ran into Erich's ex-wife, Sharon, who lived in Sedona along with their adorable little son, Chris. Sharon was quite a bit younger than Erich, making him an older father. The group hung around with them for a little while, but Dawn could tell that Sharon was pissed off at Erich for some reason, and it made everything just a little uncomfortable.

At one point, Erich made a joke about something and Dawn laughed with him. Sharon folded her arms and smirked. She said, "Oh Dawn, you're just another one in Erich's harem, aren't you? You should know better."

For some reason, everyone around Dawn kept assuming that she was hooking up with Erich. She found that weird and couldn't figure it out, especially as Dawn was notably older than Erich. Although it made Dawn's temper rise a bit, Erich whispered to her to just ignore his ex. So she did but mostly because she knew the venom was more directed towards Erich than herself anyway.

Later that night, back at the Center, Dawn was awakened by noises coming from the meditation room, and she smiled to herself. Her friends were having a good time. She was happy for them, but wished they were a little quieter about it.

From Dawn's Journal

At the Light Center, there are so many people who are seeking something in their lives. It's encouraging, actually. There are some who believe that there is a new age coming—that more people will be enlightened. If that's true, then it seems that seeking would be the most important thing a person could do. It's a comforting thought.

CHAPTER 27

"Hey there, sistahs!" shouted Dawn happily into her phone. Lola, Bea, Judith, and Helen joined in on Facetime and greeted their friend.

"How is Sedona?" asked Judith excitedly.

"Tell us everything!" yelled Helen, happily.

"Oh my Lord, I hardly know where to begin," said Dawn, rolling her eyes. "But let me just start off by saying I have never been anywhere so flat-out beautiful. Or peaceful. These red rock mountains are gorgeous. I almost killed myself coming in from the airport. I was driving when I first saw the mountains, and it was just too much. You have to come and see this."

"We can't wait to visit someday, dear," answered Bea, smiling. "Where are you staying?"

"I'm staying at a place called the Light Center. And get this— I'm sleeping in a big common room with a bunch of other people. There were probably ten other people in there all at once last night."

"What?" yelped Lola, then burst out laughing. "A group sleep-in? And I thought I was the slutty one!"

"Oh, you still are," confirmed Dawn, and the sentiment was confirmed by the other sistahs who all nodded gravely.

"Hey!" said Lola, looking around crossly. "No ganging up."

Dawn ignored her and went on, "Seriously, you should see this place, sistahs. There's art everywhere and people come here because they are all seekers. And they are drawn to Sedona because of its magical energy. Just like me."

"So you didn't sleep with anyone?" asked Lola, sounding disappointed.

"Nope, sorry to let you down, Lola. But I have to admit, there is the most handsome man staying here. His name is Erich. He checked into the center in the middle of the night and woke me up to ask where the bedding was kept. I opened my eyes and thought I was dreaming of the gods." She chuckled.

"Now, that sounds promising," said Lola, satisfied.

"Oh, just stop already. I had breakfast with him this morning, and he's such a nice person. He's here visiting from Hawaii. I like him, but it's definitely in a friend way, Lola. So just calm down. I'm not here looking for a man, and you know it. Besides, he's with a woman named Krysta."

"So, what's on the schedule today?" Helen asked, changing the subject.

"I'm seeing Sondraya today for my reading, and I just can't wait. Then tonight, Erich and Krysta invited me and a couple of other folks from the Center to join him for a channeling."

"Whatever that is," said Judith, adding, "But it sounds interesting."

Lola asked, "Are the crows surrounding the Light Center?"

"No, surprisingly enough. They're not."

Helen thought a moment and suggested, "I think we were right when we said that they don't have to remind you about anything right now because you're on the right path."

"That could be, Helen. I hope you're right. It's hard to know what I should do here, so I'm just trying everything. But look, I have to run now. I have to get ready—there's so much to do today!"

"Call me tomorrow," reminded Lola and added, "And be careful, sistah."

Dawn hung up the phone smiling, and then left the Center for her appointment with Sondraya.

CHAPTER 28

Dawn walked up the steps of Sondraya's modest, sand-colored house in western Sedona. The front porch was overflowing with pots of happily growing herbs. She saw rosemary, basil, thyme, and dill, to name a few. She loved that Sondraya and she both gardened, plus it lent a witchy feel to the place.

Just as when Dawn met her in Santa Barbara, Sondraya opened the front door wearing a long purple dress of soft material. Her dreadlocks were down to her waist, and light freckles floated above her welcoming smile.

"Come in, come in! So good to see you again!" she said, taking Dawn's hand. She led Dawn into her living room, and Dawn was happy to see that plants were everywhere inside too. Sondraya apparently had some sort of good plant juju—or a green thumb, as most call it. *Maybe that's the same thing,* mused Dawn.

Sondraya led her to a small table in front of a comfy, cornflower blue sofa. Still holding Dawn's hand, she started looking at it and reading her immediately. She asked, "How is your Sedona journey so far?"

"I've met so many people already, and I'm learning a lot," Dawn said happily.

"I know you have. I've pulled your chart for you, and I have a lot to tell you."

Dawn got comfortable, and Sondraya poured them tea from a pot she had sitting on the table. She couldn't wait to hear what Sondraya had to say.

Taking Dawn's hand again, she began, "You've come a long way in your life, Dawn. You had heavy childhood issues. You've fully processed a lot of lessons, and so now it's about you being truly done with your past—like the snake that fully sheds its skin. You have no accountability left. It's gone and done.

"You have a very strong health line in your palm. And an inner line here of protection. These are very good; it means you are being protected now. But they are there for a specific reason. Those lines don't usually show up unless you are living under a certain amount of stress and tension."

Dawn answered, "You could say that. As you know, I'm a fairly recent widow, and I feel that things are changing around me at a fast pace. I'm not sure what to make of it yet, but I have this idea. Sondraya, I have to ask you a question. It's about something that has been recently suggested to me, but I don't know if I dare to believe it. Do you think it's possible for me to do something like what you do—healing and psychic reading and such? I think I might be called to do this."

Sondraya suddenly crowed loudly, startling Dawn, "Yes! Yes! I've got the chills everywhere! Because Spirit wouldn't let me say it until you brought it up. The markings of the Psychic are right here on your palm—see! They are the markings of the Stigmata. Take a look!" she held Dawn's hand and pointed. "Yes, and yes, and yes again! You must claim this and bring it forth. And you have this marking here. It's called the ring of Solomon. And it's the gift of inspiration and the markings of a teacher. Yes! You have gifts, and you are being called to use them. It's time for you to become who you are really meant to be."

Dawn thought about that for a moment, brow furrowed. She asked, "But exactly what kind of work should I do? The Tarot was suggested to me, and then there are these visions I told you about."

Sondraya thought a moment. "Let me just look inside for a minute while you pick a tarot card on this issue…Ok, so what I'm getting is that you can do your own business by your own hand. And look, you've picked a business card. It represents communication. Hmmmm. It looks like you need to just start doing something, anything, along those lines, and Spirit will show you the way. And talking about it to people. And journaling about it. And learning everything you can. Ask for Spirit's guidance. It may be good to start with the Tarot, but your visions are very valuable. You're going to have to try all of it until Spirit lets you know which way to go. But don't sit and wait. Get into action. It's time for you to trust and take risks. Spirit is going to be the one to provide the things and the people you need to come into your life.

"Listen, I'll tell you a story. I danced around the world, and I've never even had dancing lessons! The thing is, I would go home at night after work and light candles, and I would dress up in my best beauty—like a high priestess. And I always kept mirrors around me, and I recommend this to people. I always had altars because that's where energy builds up. If you do this, always have a beautiful picture of yourself on your altar because that's what you want to evoke—your own goddess within yourself. Anyway, I just started praying. What I wanted more than anything was to be a dancer, but I didn't believe it could happen. I was well into my forties and overweight—heavier than I am now. I was too shy to even go to dancing lessons. But I would turn on music, and then I would start seeing a circle on the ceiling of my room of all my ancestors. What I saw was that there were millions of people supporting me. And millions of people that I'm here to support. It just kept going on and on. The people would come out, and they would dance, and I would dance with them. And sometimes, I would dance for eight hours straight! I loved it so much. I would go all through the night and barely make it to work the next day, or I would call in and not even go to work because I made Spirit more important than my job. I didn't do it that often. I only did it about four times. But each time it was so intense, and it was at least for four hours."

"Dawn, you need to envision what you want and start to work a little bit towards it every single day, like I did. And you can go even faster than I did. I was slow. It took me maybe a year or two for the final manifestation to let me walk into a concert venue and for a woman to notice me and ask, 'Are you an artist?' She told me to see her at the break in the music. To this day, I'm still not sure why she singled me out. When I caught up to her she said, 'I've got this little international dance company. I don't normally do this, but I'm going to show you some films of our group and what we do. And if you like it, would you join us? By the way, do you dance?' That's exactly how she put it—just out of nowhere! That's how Spirit worked!

"Three months later, I was dancing at the MGM in Reno. We danced at all the best hotels all over the US. I was getting a standing ovation from over four thousand people a night for a single dance that I did. All from prayer. From just dreaming it. Taking time to dream and dealing with intention. When you say what it is and dream about it, you let go. You let Spirit in. I didn't worry about it or try to figure out how it was all going to happen. If I had tried to figure it out I would have messed it all up. I just said, 'Spirit, I want that in my next life.' But you know, we have so many lifetimes in this one lifetime. We have so many lifetimes that are happening right here. So, you want it, you've got it. It will come to you.

"If you are experiencing frustration and depression and fear, and I think you have been, it helps to call out and take those fears someplace where you can scream. I used to go to the ocean and scream out to God, 'I want to be released. I want to be released from the fear.'

"And let me tell you, when I lived on Maui, everyone was telling me that it was impossible for me to live the way I wanted to live, and I started believing them. I wanted my own house, and I couldn't get one. I didn't have a good credit rating, and no one would rent anything decent to me. I got so depressed that I got up and went out in the middle of the night to the ocean and I asked God, 'God, what is the matter? Why do I feel depressed?' And I thought for a minute and said, 'God, I've lost faith. I'm depressed and I don't believe.' And I knew then that I really didn't believe anymore, and I was so sad about it. So I said, 'God I really don't believe. I've lost faith.' So, I asked, 'What do I do?'

"I asked, 'Where is my wisdom? What is the first thing I can do? Here I am. I'm hopelessly depressed. I don't have any faith, and I need a house. What do I do?' And then, it just came to me. I just visualized what I wanted. But I still said, 'God I don't believe you. I don't have any faith. You know what? I want a house, and I want it now!' And I imagined taking a fishing rod and casting it right over all my doubts, into the ocean. I was screaming and crying, and I wanted to be changed. I wanted all the sadness to be taken away from me right away. I said, 'Give me what is due me. Give me a house that is as beautiful—no, even more beautiful than the house I left behind.'

"And then I went home. And within twenty-four hours, I was guided to the most beautiful house I've ever seen in my life. It was a round, twelve-sided temple house. The owner didn't even ask for my credit rating. He was a Christian, so I wasn't sure how he would feel about what I did for a living. But still, when he asked for it, I gave him my business card which read, 'Readings: Palmistry, Astrology, Tarot.' He looked at me and said, 'You know what? I'm a reader of sorts too, and you're a good spirit, and I'm glad you're here.' It was so amazing!

"The biggest things that have ever come to me in my life did not come when I believed. They came when I had the biggest doubt. But I always asked for what I wanted anyway. I faced my own doubt by saying, 'I don't believe—but still give me this and that.' Once you face the doubt, and you see it, it can't stay there. Wherever we are is perfect to get us to wherever we want to be. And we use it in our prayer and in claiming."

Dawn interrupted. "You know, it feels as if I'm just starting out with my life all over again. I'm not sure where I'm going, but I'm starting over."

"Oh Sweetie! I'm a late bloomer too. I did not walk out of corporate America until I was in my late forties. So you're doing it right on time. In fact, there is no wrong time. I didn't have the courage to do it back then. You know what I think it was for me? First of all working at a job gave me a cushion. I was doing temporary work and trying to find a way to do what I love. I would work so many months out of the year and then not work for three or four months, so I wasn't too uncomfortable. But I also used to believe that the source of my income came from my job. I was very logical back then, and I really believed that. Then one day, I started claiming that God was the source of my income. I started claiming it long before I believed it. And it's just the living proof; you don't have to believe. Tell God, 'Prove it to me! Show me! Show me that you are the source. Take care of me!' And when I walked out of my job, I did not even have a big clientele for my new business. I was only working part time doing my healing work. And everybody at my old job said, 'You'll be back.' I said, 'No, I won't. I will die first.' That's my Scorpio side. I said that, 'I would die first before I go and do 'downtown' work ever again.' It's good to know what you will *not* do as much as knowing what you *will* do. It clarifies things.

"I just want to share all these stories because I believe we're all one. If it happens to me, it happens to you. This is the job I hold: to hold the dreams for people. And this is now your job too. Make sure that Spirit makes it happen."

From Dawn's Journal

I am so jacked-up from being in Sondraya's company. That woman is pure light! And she has me inspired to visualize where I'm going in this new life of mine, to call out to Spirit for it, to take baby steps, and just start heading in my new direction, and to keep going. And maybe even to think bigger. I'm starting to visualize being able to work with people back home, to help them find their purpose and elevate their own energies and lives. I can't think of anything I want to do more.

CHAPTER 29

As soon as she answered the phone, Lola demanded, "Tell me about Sondraya,"

"Lola, I wish you had been there with me. It was such an amazing experience, being seen by someone that way."

"I see you all the time!" objected Lola.

"No, not that way. I mean this woman could see my dreams and thoughts and especially my purpose."

"Wait, what? You have a purpose?"

"Gee, thanks, sistah!" Dawn answered, drily.

"I didn't mean it the way it sounded."

"I know. Listen, she told me that my life is changing all over the place and that's why I have been so antsy lately. And it's why the crows are being so damned pushy! I need to pursue my new purpose. And that purpose is to bring people along with me on a spiritual journey. I mean, think about it. What could possibly be more important to a person than getting closer to spirit, or source, or God? So, Sondraya said I should keep practicing the Tarot and visions, and whatever other tools I can find to help people find themselves. And by helping others, I'll also help me find myself."

Lola was quiet for a moment. "Dawn, I know we kid around a lot, but I can hear it in your voice that you've stumbled onto something important. So, let me just say that I will support you in what you are doing."

Dawn didn't answer for a moment as she fought back tears that were threatening to overflow. "Thanks, sistah. You know I love you too, Lola."

"Oh God, don't you dare make me cry on this phone," moaned Lola. "Go away and call me tomorrow. And don't you dare not be careful out there!"

CHAPTER 30

Ashtar

That evening, Dawn treated everyone in the Light Center by cooking up a big pot of Chicken Etouffee. She loved watching their faces as they sampled Louisiana cooking, some for the first time. Everyone became immediate fans.

Later that night Erich and Krysta invited her to join them at a meeting with a well-known channeler. A channeler was apparently someone who is able to allow other beings to speak and act through them. It sounded fascinating to Dawn, and she couldn't wait to see what would happen.

The meeting was held at the home of a local psychiatrist who had a reputation in Sedona as a highly evolved being. He greeted everyone at the door with a huge hug. As they moved past him, Erich whispered to Dawn, "Did you feel that? When you hug him, he doesn't even feel solid, almost like he is not entirely on the planet."

The chairs in the large living room were placed in a semi-circle and every seat was taken with about thirty people of a wide demographic of ages and ethnicities.

Quiet music was playing as they took their seats. The host began with leading a group meditation. He talked to the group about how things were getting ready to change. He said that there was some dimensional work going on and certain people were going into the fourth dimension. Dawn felt very relaxed and meditative, and safe.

Then a woman came in dressed in a long, white gown. She was the guest of honor, and she told them that she was channeling a being called Ashtar. She explained that Ashtar is a leader and messenger from the Light Board, the governing board of the universe under God's command. She sat at the front of the room and went into a short trance. Then, she came awake suddenly and became powerful and strong looking, almost warrior-like in demeanor. She said, "I will stand," and did. She walked about the room, looking at everyone. Her hands were placed proudly on her hips, and she was telling everyone that they had beautiful faces and what lovely beings they were. She was riveting and her face was radiant.

Ashtar's message was about loving one another, being faithful to love, and becoming open to ritual. She talked about the future. She said that communities would be springing up to move the evolving beings forward, and they should watch for them.

Dawn enjoyed the evening though she didn't understand it all. This was brand new material for her. What she did understand was that everyone in the room, everyone everywhere, was searching, experimenting, and learning, and that they were all connected. They were all one. And they were all evolving. But seekers do not always encounter truth, and Dawn felt that people have to learn to use their own instincts to sense what is true—even if it is only true for them. Dawn felt there were definitely some truths in the messaging tonight.

Ashtar led a guided meditation and instructed the group to picture themselves standing on her spaceship. Dawn thought she would feel silly doing this, but she immediately fell into a vision and found herself on that ship, flying away from the earth at an incredible speed, going farther and farther away during the meditation. It was an extremely vivid vision for her and different from her usual. Perhaps because it was another vision that she had commanded to happen. It reaffirmed that she could bring on a vision, and that other people could also command one from her too, if she was receptive to it. Dawn found that just fascinating.

Ashtar asked the group if they had any questions and they did, including things like: Will the third dimension still be here when we move to the fourth dimension? Ashtar said yes, it would be. They exist at the same time.

At that moment, something remarkable and unexpected happened. Mid-sentence, Ashtar stopped what she was doing and stared. She raised her arm into the air and pointed across the room—right at Dawn. Dawn was a little alarmed at first. She didn't particularly like being made a spectacle of in a crowd of people. She cringed inwardly with dread. She hoped like heck that Ashtar wasn't going to ask her to volunteer for something in front of everyone. But that didn't happen. Instead, Ashtar said, "My dear, you have a glowing, purple, heart-shaped aura. It's simply beautiful." Everyone in the room turned to stare at Dawn, and she felt her face turning crimson.

Then, fortunately, the speaker moved on with her talk

Dawn, of course, did not hear one word of the rest of what the speaker had to say that evening. She didn't know what a purple, heart-shaped aura signified, but she knew it meant something, and that it was a damned-good something, at that. She still had so much to learn.

She smiled to myself and felt oddly proud about something she didn't understand and had no control over, which made her laugh. She thought, *"Who cares if I don't understand—I have a purple, heart-shaped aura! Lola's aura will be green with envy!"*

From Dawn's Journal:

Tonight was so strange! I'm not sure why Ashtar singled me out, but I can't help but feel that she had sent a sign through the Channeler that I am doing the right things and guiding my life to something more meaningful. I am beginning to learn to trust the signs—and I believe that is no small feat.

CHAPTER 31

"**S**he said you had a heart-shaped aura? Are you sure she was talking to you?" asked Lola skeptically.

"Yes, I'm sure," answered Dawn with a sigh.

"I would have thought it was shaped more like a caution sign. Or maybe a big question mark."

Dawn laughed and said, "I was hoping for a fleur de lis shape myself."

"But I guess a heart makes sense," added Lola, teasingly. "You're just a big puddle of love these days. And speaking of love, how is Erich doing? The Sistahs and I are calling him the Hunky Hawaiian."

"Erich is great. He's turning out to be a good friend, thank you very much. Plus, once again, he's with Krysta. They've been hanging out together a lot."

"Oh well, don't give up," sighed Lola.

"Oh, you give up—please! I'm not here for Erich, or George, or John, or any other guy and you know it. I don't need any distractions, but I admit, I am enjoying all the company."

"So what's on the agenda today?"

Dawn said excitedly, "I went hiking in the red hills early this morning. There are such strong energy centers, and it was amazing to meditate on top of those powerful places."

"I can't believe you get to experience all this, Dawn."

"I'm planning to take a quick side trip to see the Grand Canyon in a couple of days. I've never seen it."

"It all sounds so awesome. Send lots of picture and call me tomorrow and tell me more. And for God's sake, don't you fall in that canyon!"

CHAPTER 32

Stories from the Light Center

Guests wandered in an out of the Light Center on a daily basis, and it was a great adventure for Dawn to meet them all. Dawn had to admit that the Center didn't attract the same type of person that she'd be likely to meet on the main street of Covington, Louisiana. Many of the guests were in the healing business, or artists, or something equally interesting.

For instance:

Elke and Nelson

One morning, a new couple arrived at the Center. The woman, Elke, was a tall, plump, black woman with short, black dreadlocks and an extraordinary presence. She spoke loudly and excitedly, and every once in a while, let out with a loud "Whoop!" Her boyfriend, Nelson, was older than Elke, in his late fifties, thin, somewhat stooped but with a friendly nature. They were talking excitedly about a meeting they had attended the night before with a man called the Tooth Fairy, of all things. The man claimed to be an alchemist, and said he could change the mercury fillings in a person's mouth to gold. Elke and Nelson were showing everyone who wanted to see their new gold fillings that they said were not there the day before. Dawn found herself peering into their mouths along with everyone else. That was certainly something she had never pictured herself doing before.

From Dawn's Journal:

I didn't know what to make of that. Elke and Nelson looked so excited, and they obviously believed that it was true. Who do I believe? Why not believe everything? Or nothing? Certainly, I was here to be open to possibilities, but my conservative background holds me in check at times. I decided not to worry about it. Judging the people here was the last thing I wanted to do, no matter how crazy they sounded (oops). Just as I did when people told me they were from Jupiter, I filed this new piece of alchemy information away with all the rest of the things I wasn't really sure about. Worrying about all that would constitute falling too much on the conservative side of the fence. It felt right to just be OK with what was happening, to listen, to acknowledge other people's beliefs and spirits, and then let it sit. I need to stay focused and take in what is most important. I figured I would assimilate new things as I went along.

❖❖❖

Erich

Erich is the Adonis from Maui or the Hunky Hawaiian, as Lola called him, and Dawn's new friend. He was definitely one of the more interesting ones. He was born in Germany, and his family once owned a castle there. When Germany became nationalized, the family lost the property and castle. Now that the Germany's borders were open again, his family was able to get the castle back, but they don't know what to do with it. It has enormous upkeep for which they were quite unprepared. Erich looks aristocratic. There is something in his carriage and even in his aquiline nose that screams nobility and a fancy family tree. Dawn spent a lot of time hanging around with him because he was good company—kind, funny and almost always in a good mood.

One night he came back to the center and asked Dawn if she wanted to talk outside on the deck for a while. He had spent the afternoon with his little son, Chris, and he seemed uncharacteristically down in the mouth. She agreed, and they both wrapped blankets around themselves and went outside on the cold deck to talk.

He told her that in Maui, people he knew were very happy and self-sufficient. Everything grows so easily out there. There is fruit to pick right off the trees. It's paradise. The problem that he faced now was that his son lived in Sedona with his mother. Erich was here to visit him, but he would have to return home soon and leave Chris behind. It was just breaking his heart to have to do this.

Dawn had watched Erich with his son around the Center and at the arts festival, and she told him how wonderful it was to see him as a father. She told him that it was easy to tell that he cared for his son greatly. He was a good father and Chris would need him while growing up. She suggested that he try to stay in town for a while, that even if he did go back, he needed to get Chris to come out and see him often. Erich needed to give as much love as he could to his son. Dawn told him, "Don't hold back, even if it hurts. The boy needs your love."

Then she gave him a hug and told him that he needed to sleep on the matter and something would come to him in the morning. She was getting flashes of vision for him. They were tiny visions of Erich and his son together, smiling, and she told him about it. He nodded with understanding. It wasn't the first time he had encountered someone with psychic gifts, which was a relief to Dawn. She felt that she could trust him to accept her gifts, and she was right. And she also knew that she was right in her advice to him.

The next afternoon, she found Erich in the main room of the Center with Chris. Erich told her that he had decided to stay in Sedona for a while. Dawn was delighted for both of them. Erich was smiling and had his arm around his beautiful little, long haired boy. He was so gentle with Chris. He told Dawn that his decision was because of their conversation. He had slept on the matter and realized in his dreams that there was no way he could leave his boy at that time. He would look for work in Sedona and find a way. He seemed very relieved. Dawn was sure everything would work out for him.

She felt good at having helped Erich. She had never before given advice after having a vision for someone. She had never even told anyone that she'd had a vision about them. She told Erich, and he listened, and it helped him. Sondraya was right. This was what Dawn was meant to do, help people with her gift. It felt so right.

Later in the evening, she went for a walk with Erich. They walked up the road in the dark and looked at the amazing amount of stars in the sky. He told her about a UFO that he had seen once while camping outside of Page, Arizona. Erich was a pilot back in Hawaii, and he said that he'd seen many odd things, but he'd never seen anything like that UFO before. He was by himself at the camping grounds when he saw a light coming over the horizon. He thought at first it was an airplane but it began to do some very un-airplane-like things, things even a helicopter can't do. The light suddenly came closer to him. At that moment he began to feel very uncomfortable and afraid. Then the light suddenly disappeared. He was convinced it was a UFO. His instincts told him that the beings on the UFO had somehow sensed his fear, and it made them retreat. He felt they were benevolent and he was convinced that if he had welcomed them in his mind and told them to come closer, that they would have.

They talked about many things that night. Dawn told Erich that she would like to work as a psychic reader someday. Erich listened, then he told her that people often came to him for guidance when they had a business idea. He has good business sense, and people trust his judgment. He said that often he could tell immediately that some of those people would not succeed. He never told tell them that outright because he doesn't like to hurt feelings or quell people's creativity, but tries to gently point them in a different direction. He doesn't feel like he is supposed to deprive people of certain lessons they need to learn, but he tries to hint about what would serve them better. He told Dawn that, without a doubt, she would succeed in whatever she did. He told her that she has the kind of energy that succeeds. She loved hearing that from him and took it to heart. It was very encouraging. But if she was being honest, she didn't think of it as a business—just a calling.

Then Dawn mentioned to him that she was making a bead necklace to remind her of her trip to Sedona. She had collected beautiful, multi-colored beads and charms from different places along the way to slowly add to the necklace. She had charms representing angels, snakes, spiral vortexes, crosses, suns, and moons and many beads. Erich stopped short in the road, smiling, and reached into his pocket He pulled out a little, soft pouch and poured a handful of beads into his palm He told her to pick two of them for her necklace. She was amazed. He told her that he only gave them out to people he liked. Dawn couldn't believe the coincidence. Then she remembered, of course, that there are no coincidences, especially on this trip. Still, she was deeply touched. He told her, "Dawn, my friend, there's something so innocent and open about you. The universe cannot help but love you." Dawn felt that that was such a beautiful thing to say to someone. Her whole trip was adding meaning to her life, and she knew it with every fiber in her body.

The next night, Erich invited her to go with him and Krysta to hear a man named Jonanda speak at the New Age Center. Since she was in Sedona to experience everything she could, she accepted, and they drove together in Dawn's rental car. Jonanda turned out to be an older man with white hair, dressed entirely in khaki, with a cheerful, cherubic grin. He was tall, thin, and originally from Copenhagen. He seemed a very peaceful, kind man with a sweet nature. He spoke about how we are all a part of a hierarchy of beings, and that we'd come down to this planet for different lives. He said that before arriving on this planet, we looked around and chose our parents, our lives, and our purpose. He also said that we came down in different forms, not just human. Jonanda said that thousands of years ago, other beings lived here as well as humans. He said that he had been alive at the time in a different life form and that the other beings attacked him. One of them hit Jonanda in the middle of his back, and it shocked him so much that, to this day, and he still retains pain from it. He said that we all have a responsibility to come down to earth to create a place of unconditional love so that we could heal the planet and change it. Dawn found him very inspiring. What he taught was certainly different from everything Dawn had been exposed to, and she was ready to listen.

The next morning, Dawn and Erich left early went to a breakfast meeting of the Light Net, as they called themselves. They are a network of "light people" and healers from all over the world. They met at the Coffee Pot restaurant, and Dawn met, among others, Christopher James, who was the founder, and his girlfriend, Gaia. Christopher mentioned that he was sixty, and Gaia must have been about forty. Dawn got a chance to talk a little to Gaia and found her interesting. She used to work as an office assistant in Los Angeles when she met Christopher. Afterwards, she sold everything she owned, and they moved to Sedona, and she had never been happier. They stayed with people and lived in tents for a while until they found a permanent home. One of her friends, a commercial artist from Denmark, still lived here in a tent. Christopher and Gaia made their living as psychic healers. For the Light Net group, Erich volunteered to be a contact for them in Maui. Dawn put her name in too for a Louisiana contact. These were people living their lives out of the box and open to the universe, and Dawn found them inspiring.

On a walk later that evening, Dawn told Erich that she thought he must be one of God's blessed. Everything seemed to come so easily to him. Everyone seemed to love him. She couldn't help but admire that. He told her that he hadn't always been that way. He said that when his son was born, he and his wife had named him Christopher Angel Michael. Erich felt that Chris had come into his life in order to open his father's heart. And that's exactly what the boy had done. One day, Erich asked Chris, "Why are you here?" And the little boy had said to his daddy, "To help you." It blew Erich away and he learned a lot about love from his boy. He told Dawn that he strived to become love, and that we were all love. And that nothing that we could do was unrelated to love in some way—not even murder, not war—nothing. It was all love in its own way. He said that life is very simple. Everything is provided for us that we need. He had faith in it. And the more he had faith in it, the more it became true. "There's two things to remember" he said, "Trust and relax."

From Dawn's Journal:

Trust and Relax. To think that there are people going through life in so much peace. I just love that about Erich. Another thing I like about him is that I feel safe with him. He does not come on to me, and I appreciate it. He even calls me "Sister." Lola thinks there might be something going on between us, but it is only a lovely friendship, and that is such a gift, one that I wish was not so rare. Erich is beautiful and a warm-hearted soul, and I know that I will never forget him. His life is so simple. So peaceful. So evolved. I'm lucky to know him.

✦✦✦✦✦✦

Anthony

Anthony was a self-described energy worker from Los Angeles. One afternoon, he taught Dawn about the I Ching, which is an ancient form of Chinese divination. She spent a couple of hours with him learning to do a reading with this tool and thought it was fascinating. Anthony happened to mention during their talk that he had an opening in the top of his head because his fontanel had never quite closed up. He said it allowed him to channel energy in through his crown chakra and healing came through him in this way. He told her to touch the top of his head and, sure enough, there was a big indentation. Dawn felt a little creeped out by it. Then she slowly realized that she was getting a little creeped out by Anthony altogether because, to Dawn's surprise, he started acting like he was attracted to Dawn and was up for a little vacation romance. But she simply wanted to spend some time with him and learn from him. He was good-looking and charismatic, but Dawn wasn't up for it. That's not why she was on her trip. However, her rejection of him did not go over well, and she sensed his anger. So she cut short their talk and tried to stay away from him.

But one evening, Dawn sat on a bench in a hallway at the Center for privacy as she called her daughter. While she was on the phone Anthony walked by and heard her talking. He suddenly grabbed Dawn and started tickling her fiercely. There was nothing playful about it. It was nothing short of a physical attack. She could feel his anger, and it was surprisingly strong. He was trying to get even with her for rejecting him. Dawn was shocked and pushed him away. He stopped, but he walked away snickering. After that, Dawn avoided him completely. He brooded around the Center, coming in and out for a couple of days and then left, and she was relieved when he did.

From Dawn's Journal:

I think that anyone who takes this kind of journey needs to be careful and trust their instincts. Anthony was a perfect example of why that is the case. I trusted him at first, but then his true colors started to come through. Thank God, I was able to stay away from him, and thank God he left. I hope he finds help for his anger problems.

Maya

Maya was Paul's girlfriend. She had her own cute, little geodesic dome cabin and studio out in back of the Light Center all to herself. Maya was an artist, and several of her paintings hung in the Center. She was in her thirties and very beautiful with long shiny brown hair. Dawn wasn't sure of her ethnicity, but guessed that she was of Asian or maybe Native American descent. She was tanned, lean with long hair, and she had an angular face. She wasn't unpleasant, but not overly friendly and kept to herself most of the time. There was definitely an air of mystery about her.

After dinner one night, Maya invited several people in the Center to what she called a Toning in the meditation room. Dawn didn't know what a Toning was, so she accepted the invitation. It was so unusual for Maya to speak to anyone that Dawn was curious to see what she was about. Five guests, including Dawn, gathered for the session. They sat against the walls in the round room on brightly-colored pillows, and Maya stood in the middle. She told everyone that they could expect some strange sounds in the room and that they should just experience them and not worry. Dawn didn't know what to make of that, but she was ready for anything. Then Maya turned down the lights and had everyone do some breathing exercises. They were breathing deeply and relaxing when suddenly, unearthly sounds began to come from Maya's mouth. She was moaning and growling and sounded like an assortment of wild animals. It was incredible. She had great lung capacity and was able to hold the sounds for a long time. The guests glanced at each other, some questioning, some amazed. Dawn was thrilled and thought it was astoundingly cool. Then Maya began to sing. She sounded like whales from far away oceans communicating with each other. Then she sang what she called "Adult Lullabies." She sang in a language that was Maya's alone. The songs were haunting. She turned around at one point, looked right at Dawn and sang one of her songs to her. The range of her voice was remarkable, and her capacity was astounding. Instead of closing her eyes Dawn looked deep into Maya's and attempted to communicate with her to enhance the experience. She found it difficult though. It was almost as if Maya wasn't human anymore. When it was over, Maya left them without saying very much, maintaining her mysterious persona. The guests discussed the experience with each other. Richard, one of the other guests, said that what he saw was a woman who turned into a Native American brave and then a wolf. A shape-shifter. Dawn felt that he had hit it right on the nose—Maya was definitely shifting something about herself right in front of their eyes. It was an astounding experience, but Dawn had no idea what it meant except to say that maybe she should not count on what she sees every day as being real.

The next day, Dawn ran into Maya in the main room. She told her how much she had enjoyed the Toning session, and Dawn asked to see her art work. Maya seemed happy to bring out her work to show, and the art did not disappoint. The painting she was currently working on showed trees morphing into people and dragons. It was brilliantly colored and detailed. There were several other smaller works that Maya called dream paintings. They looked like Maya's music sounded, with flowing leaves and spirals of hearts. Maya remained a mystery to Dawn, but she couldn't help but admire her work.

From Dawn's Journal:

I ended up buying a print of one of Maya's dream paintings. I got the impression that she could use some money, and I wanted to help her out monetarily and also have something to remind me of her and the Center. By buying her work, Maya said that we were contributing to each other's dreams. She was very happy about the sale, and I love the piece—a glimpse into that mysterious woman's soul.

Naomi

Naomi is the woman who worked at the Center in exchange for her stay there since her boyfriend tossed her out of their apartment. She was also one of the dearest people Dawn had ever met. Her spirit was so calm and sweet, even though she'd had a hard life. Naomi had nothing to her name. If it wasn't for the Center, she might very well be homeless.

Dawn told Naomi that she was worried about her. She couldn't imagine what it was like to have no place to go. Naomi was calm and almost Buddha-like. She said, "I have food, I have a place to stay, and I have work. I was supposed to come here, and I am supposed to stay here for now. So I will be here and not worry about it." Her way of looking at life blew Dawn away. Dawn thought her a great teacher. She gave Naomi a bit of money one day to help her out, and Naomi accepted it gratefully in her usual, beautiful style.

One day, a friend of Naomi's came to visit her. His name was Jack the Frenchman; at least that's what Naomi told Dawn. She introduced him, and he came straight up to Dawn and kissed her right on the mouth. She was completely shocked and gaped at him. "What the hell?" she sputtered. But Naomi started laughing with delight, and Jack just grinned and said, "Well, what did you expect from a Frenchman?" The pair of them were so cute about their prank that Dawn couldn't even be mad about it. If it had happened anywhere else, she would have been furious. She thought to herself, "*It's all in the intention.*" She still picked up a throw pillow and whacked him with it, laughing.

Later, Naomi took Dawn aside because she wanted to show her a collection of little drawings she had done of women with flowing hair and carnival masks. There were all sorts of women—beautiful goddesses and dangerous-looking vamps. There were fairies and female creatures emerging from fluffy clouds. Dawn was delighted with her obvious talent and suggested that maybe Naomi could sell the pictures. They weren't exactly portraits, but they were impressions that Naomi received from the people she drew. Dawn thought the name of the drawings could be "Soul Sketches." She already knew that Naomi was a very intuitive person, but looking at her pictures, she realized that there was much more to Naomi than she had even imagined. She was a reader of sorts too, and she certainly had an artist's talent.

Dawn suggested that people might hire Naomi to sketch their inner soul and the interpretation of it. Naomi listened with interest, then she offered to let Dawn choose one of her sketches to keep. Dawn picked the one of a fairy emerging from the clouds. She felt it represented transformation. It was such a light and happy picture that she wanted to keep it to remind her of Naomi and this transforming time. Naomi then asked Dawn to repay her by drawing a picture of her. She offered Dawn her pastels and sketch pad. Dawn looked at her with her eyes widened. She was more than a little surprised. She didn't draw very well and knew nothing about working with pastels. But Naomi said to just keep the materials with her that day and something would come to her. She seemed to have all the confidence Dawn lacked.

Dawn walked away slowly, wondering what she could possibly draw, and then she stopped short. Naomi was right. Something was coming to her in the form of an immediate vision. She stood in the hallway receiving the message. Afterwards, she went and sat peacefully in the garden, and about a half an hour later, gave Naomi a drawing of her vision. It was a sketch of a cupped hand and inside the hand sat a pixie, a kind of butterfly person. It was Naomi with large purple, butterfly wings. Surrounding her was a yellow light, and outside the hand was an ominous dark green. She drew Naomi as an emerging, beautiful chrysalis who was protected in a tough period of time and staying in a secure home that was mostly made of love. Naomi was overwhelmed by the picture. She told Dawn that the butterfly had always been her symbol and her totem, and that she did feel protected in her life. As for Dawn, she surprised herself by the whole experience. She had no idea that she could produce a picture like that, and she felt wonderful giving a meaningful gift to her friend.

From Dawn's Journal:

I gave Naomi my contact information for when I go back to Covington. I can't help but worry what will happen to her eventually. Although, I have to admire the fact that Naomi doesn't seem all that worried at all about it. I think she follows Erich's motto—trust the universe and relax. Would that I could follow that advice!

Bob

Dawn met Bob, an Oncologist from Phoenix, briefly while eating lunch one day at the Center. He told her that he had gone to the Airport vortex that day, one of the better known energy centers in Sedona. She told Bob that she had been at the same vortex just that morning. He said that the experience had shaken him. In fact, it had made him cry. Dawn told him that actually, it had made her a little sick. And it had. Her stomach had started hurting terribly while she was there. And it wasn't the first time that this had happened to her. There's something about the vortices that made her stomach vibrate and become nauseated. She told him that she had cried too, but mostly because she felt physically terrible. In fact, she still felt a little out of it.

That afternoon, Dawn still wasn't feeling quite right. She was so tired. She hadn't been sleeping well in the Center from all the bodies sleeping in one room. She felt completely drained and just wanted to fall over. So she sat down in the middle of the main floor at the Center, leaned against her bedroll and fell right to sleep sitting up.

Bob came in later, and after Dawn had woken up, he said to her, "You are amazing. I watched you, and you were in the most incredibly deep meditation that I've had ever seen." He was dead serious. Dawn just started laughing, but never told him the truth. It was too funny.

From Dawn's Journal:

Lola is going to love this story. I miss her and can't wait to see the Sistahs again soon. But I'm very happy to be here by myself at the same time. It wouldn't be the same kind of trip if Lola was here. I would be trying to meditate, and that crazy woman would be cracking jokes. Still, I miss my friends.

✦✦✦✦✦

Paul

Paul, the owner of the Center, was interesting. Dawn got all sorts of mixed signals from him. Sometimes he seemed knowledgeable and caring but at other times brooding and angry. One thing though, he was a fount of information about Sedona, Native American customs, and healing arts.

One day, he showed Dawn the medicine wheel that was in the garden. It was built with enormous, beautiful crystals that sparkled in the afternoon sun. There was a huge amethyst geode in the center. He told her that there was a woman who lived in Sedona many years ago who used to go around building medicine wheels in different parts of town, including the one in the garden, and then she would hold ceremonies. Over the years, each of the stones in the original wheel had been replaced with large crystals as gifts from various visitors to the Center.

He told her that medicine wheels were used for healing, and that there were many different types of ceremonies performed with them. The one in his garden was supposed to open the heart to love. The four spokes that came out from the wheel center represented the four directions. In a ceremony, you were supposed to walk around the outer circle and then enter from the east and sit in the middle where the healing takes place. Afterwards, you leave from the west. Once a medicine wheel is used, you are supposed to destroy it in order to destroy whatever evil or sickness that was haunting you. This wheel was too beautiful to destroy and held too much beautiful energy. So it stayed on as a beautiful sculpture in Paul's garden. Dawn thought she would like to build a medicine wheel when she got back home.

As interesting as he was, there was one thing about Paul that was disconcerting. He held odd expectations from the people on arranged work stays at his Center—like Naomi.

One day, Dawn came back to the Center from hiking and found Naomi looking perplexed and stressed. Paul had her hopping from room to room with chores. He had her pull out and switch the old refrigerator for the new one in the kitchen. Then she stripped beds and did laundry. She shook rugs and dusted. Then Paul told her that she needed to fix the leaky fixtures in the downstairs shower. That last one stopped Naomi in her tracks. She was dumbfounded, and she whispered in passing to Dawn, giggling, "Do I look like a plumber to you? I have no idea how to fix bathroom fixtures!" Paul told her that it was an easy job, and that she needed to get some Allen wrenches from the tool shed for the job. She didn't know what an Allen wrench was and didn't get a chance to ask Paul before he ran to get a phone call.

Naomi took Dawn aside and told her, "I know what a pipe wrench is. And a monkey wrench. But an Allen wrench? Was that a Woody Allen wrench or a Steve Allen wrench? I have no clue!" She laughed good-naturedly and added, "Maybe I'll go to the tool shed and all of the wrenches will be in one place and whatever I don't recognize might be an Allen wrench." Later she told me, "Well, I tried that but it didn't work. Finally, I asked Ralph, our new guest from Washington, and he told me that Allen wrenches were little 'L' shaped doodads. So, I went to the shed, found a couple of those and took them back into the bathroom. I sat looking at those wrenches and the shower fixture for about ten minutes. Guess what? Looking does absolutely no good. You have to act in order to plumb, but I have been promoted past my abilities. I'm a little embarrassed that I couldn't help. It's too bad I couldn't figure it out and surprise Paul, but that isn't going to happen today. So I did the next best thing. I left the wrenches for Paul to deal with." She laughed and added with a wink, "Life is way too short to worry about Allen wrenches."

From Dawn's Journal:

I know nothing about Paul's background, but he talks like a clipped, fast-talking northeastern boy. He's smart, abrupt, and savvy. I picture him coming from some sort of business background, then having some sort of epiphany and finding Sedona and a new way of life. I'd bet there's an interesting story there.

CHAPTER 33

Dawn laughed into the phone. "I couldn't tell him I was sleeping after all that, Lola!"

Lola could barely stop laughing, and she croaked out the words, "You mean to tell me that you were sitting up and sound asleep, and everyone thought you were in deep meditation?"

"I know! And Bob was praising me so much for my deep trance that I didn't have the heart to correct him." Dawn was now laughing so hard tears were forming.

"They're gonna make you their guru if you're not careful. Maybe make a little statue of you for garden ornaments."

"But other than that, I'm having an extraordinary time. I did a Toning exercise with a woman at the Center, then the owner, Paul, told me all about the beautiful medicine wheel in the backyard. I swear, you could feel the energy just pulsing from that thing. We have to build one. The Sistahs can all hold ceremonies in it."

"You're going to have us doing all kinds of crazy stuff when you get back."

"Yes, I am, sistah. So get ready!"

CHAPTER 34

"**L**ynn, it's Dawn."

"Well, hello there, girlfriend!"

Lynn's warm voice on the phone lightened Dawn's heart. That day, she was feeling a bit down. She was out in Sedona, making her way around in a rather blind fashion and starting to doubt what she was doing. But hearing Lynn's voice made her immediately feel right with the world. She was beginning to feel a friendship with the woman, and knew it was an unlikely occurrence, but couldn't help but feel drawn to her all the same.

Lynn was so warm and funny, and they had so much in common. Dawn truly had mixed feelings about it all. Obviously, she still had to work out her issues with Lynn about Dan, and that would probably end their relationship anyway, but something inside her hoped it wouldn't.

She told Lynn about the Toning session she'd done with Maya and about the other people she had met in the Center.

Before they got off the phone, Lynn advised her to keep doing what she was doing—meditating on the red mountains and talking to as many people as she could in Sedona because she needed to gather all the information that she could in order to discern what was true. She told Dawn that the earth was changing and our energies were changing with it, and that we all needed to do our part to support the changes.

Dawn was emotional when she said, "Thank you, Lynn. I can't wait to see you when I get back home." She got off the phone exhilarated and ready to keep moving forward in her quest.

CHAPTER 35

In a Pig's Eye

Sunrise comes late in Sedona. Arizona doesn't adhere to daylight savings time so the sun comes up at around seven o'clock AM at that time of year.

Dawn went out for an early walk around the Center's neighborhood one morning. It was cold, and her athletic shoes crunched on the icy rocks in the street. She rounded a curve and noticed an interesting sculpture of a javelina in the middle of an empty lot. She stopped to admire it for a moment.

Lawn sculptures differ in many parts of the country. In California, you see dolphin statues. In Louisiana, you see pelicans and deer. In Arizona, you see a lot of coyotes and javelinas. Many houses up and down the street sported a little critter statue or two, but Dawn wondered who had placed the statue in the middle of a vacant lot.

Then, the sculpture moved. And it snorted. Dawn froze. Two other javelinas joined the first, and one of them was a baby. It was tiny and adorable, or it would have been, except that it represented a clear and present danger. Dawn had heard that javelinas were shy animals but could become as vicious as wild boars if they thought their babies were threatened. She didn't move a single muscle. She did not want that mama javelina to feel threatened one bit.

The biggest javelina turned towards her. He faced off, snorting and pawing the ground and running back and forth. That was enough for Dawn. She gave up, turned, and ran down the street as fast as she could, all the way back to the house.

She slammed the door to the Center, adrenalin pumping in her body like a jackhammer. Once she caught her breath, she looked up javelinas in a spirit animal book, just out of curiosity, to see what a sighting of the animal meant to the Native Americans. The book didn't have anything on javelinas, but they did have the boar. Dawn thought, *"Oh I know all about boars. Boars are people who go on and on about nothing at cocktail parties."* She giggled quietly at her own joke. What it really said was that boars represented facing your fears. The book said that if a boar had come into her life today, that she was to stand up and face what she was afraid of and go forward bravely.

She thought, *"That makes sense. I came to Sedona to learn about spirituality and figure out what my visions were telling me. Was I afraid of what I might find? Was I afraid I couldn't work with people properly? Oh yes, undoubtedly so."*

She felt comforted that the javelinas had brought her a message. She was determined to stand up to her fears that day like a big pig. Something like that.

Later, she found out that javelinas aren't related to boars at all. They are part of the peccary family and are actually related to the hippopotamus. Oh well. The lesson still fit the moment.

That evening Dawn went to Bell Rock for a short hike. Bell Rock is one of the vortices and a distinctive landmark in Sedona. It looks just like its name—like a giant red bell. Some people believe that there is a space ship buried under Bell Rock awaiting a future time to emerge and do something spectacular. Dawn didn't know about that, but she did know that is a one of the most beautiful spots on earth.

The weather was cool, and she felt alive and strong while hauling herself up the red boulders. Suddenly, two young men came out of nowhere and passed her, going up the mountain. They were laughing, and she paused to watch them climb.

They were wiry Native Americans with their shirts off and their bodies tanned and strong. They were literally running up the mountain, laughing, leaping, flying from rock to rock, obviously competing with one another. Dawn could tell that the idea of their game was to climb in a continuous, fluid motion, ever upward, not stopping till they reached the top. It was amazing to watch their beautiful display of grace, youth, and strength. They looked like gazelles. Laughing gazelles. Their life force was so strong. It made Dawn feel more alive to look at them.

On her way back down, she carefully circled the big rock, finding the easiest paths down. She came around a curve just as the sun was starting to set and gasped at what she saw. On an outcropping of red rock was a young woman in a long, elegant white dress. She stood next to a man in a tuxedo, and a preacher stood in front of them, marrying them. They were backlit and glowing among one of the most gorgeous views in America. Dawn watched them for just a second, awestruck, and sad, thinking of how much she missed Dan and how much he would have loved this view. She hoped that he had the chance to see Bell Rock at sunset too. Then, she turned and left the couple to their privacy. She couldn't help but wonder if the bride wore heels to climb up the mountain. Now that would be impressive.

From Dawn's Journal:

If I could go back and do it all again, I would marry Dan again—this time at sunset on Bell Rock. It's the most romantic thing I've ever seen.

CHAPTER 36

"Lola, I went to Bell Rock, one of my favorite vortices, and I saw a bride and groom getting married at sunset. I'm telling you, I've never seen a more beautiful ceremony."

"I guess you'll have to get married again, Dawn. I want to see that wedding!"

"Sure, Lola," Dawn answered sarcastically, "I'll be sure to do that, just for you."

CHAPTER 37

awn got in her car. She was looking forward to a day trip from Sedona to see the Grand Canyon. She drove through Flagstaff on the way, a cute college town at about six thousand feet in elevation. A woman in a bagel store there told her that they get about five or six months of snow every year. She said that it was not uncommon to have their Easter egg hunts indoors because you really can't hide the eggs in snow. Dawn thought, *"Well, you CAN, but maybe a little too well."*

Her next stop on the road was a tiny chapel on the side of the highway north of Flagstaff. She pulled over to see what it was because it looked like some sort of Hobbit dwelling. It had a triangular front to it and was made of raw wooden beams and fairy dust, so it seemed. It was out in the middle of nowhere, surrounded by forest. Inside was a low ceiling and rustic wood walls, like a log cabin. It didn't seat more than about fifteen or twenty people stuck together with glue. There was a big glass window at the front with a cross built into it. Lining the walls were little pieces of paper, stuck in the cracks all over the place. Dawn was curious as to what they were so she pulled out a couple of them. They turned out to be notes, or prayers, from people that had visited the chapel. The notes were both sad and beautiful. *"Dear God, Please keep my family together this year for the sake of my son." "Lord, thank you for the past two years of holy marriage." "Thank you for the opportunity of putting us in the position where we can at last help people."* And Dawn's personal favorite, *"May the force be with you."* Realizing that she had no business reading these, she put them back where she had found them as best as she could.

On her way out, she signed the guest book and noticed a small sign attached to it. It read, *"Please, I would like to reserve this chapel for my wedding on Nov. 26th at 10AM. If you have any questions about this, please let me know. Sue."* Dawn could imagine a beautiful, little wedding in the chapel.

It was a gorgeous little spot that felt full of love. Dawn wrote a note of her own and stuck it in the wall. She thanked God for letting her find such a beautiful little corner of his world.

Next, back on the road she passed a whole forest of white Shaking Aspen trees whose leaves had turned gold for the fall. She stopped and listened to the forest talk to her. It felt like it was full of spirits that reveled in nature's beauty at work.

She made a stop at a gas station where they sold tequila flavored lollipops with worms in them. She asked the lady behind the counter about them and was told, "Yeah, they're great. They're all natural, they have no alcohol, they're sugar free, and they have protein built in."

Dawn was horrified and couldn't help but blurt out, "Yeah, but who in their right mind would eat one?"

The woman laughed at her revulsion and said, "My son would—he loves them!"

Dawn looked around in a trading post that adjoined the little gas station. It sold some of the strangest items: cow skulls, coyote fur, and various teeth, bones and hides. It occurred to her that the ultimate souvenir from the store was dried road kill. It looked like a nightmare to her.

She finally reached the Grand Canyon that afternoon. Dawn stared at the huge chasm. Then she stared some more. She looked at it from every angle she could, but no matter what she did, it just didn't look real. It looked like one big post card. It was so huge, so awesome, and it went on forever. It was an impossible thing to capture in her mind, and it felt somehow impossible to even look at. She sat contemplating it for a while then ended up leaving after just an hour. It might be one of nature's grandest views, but Dawn actually found it frustrating. She finally decided that it might, in fact, be a giant commissioned work of art, like from one of those guys who hangs gigantic curtains from bridges. She took a lot of pictures, but knew it wouldn't do any good. It was hard enough to accept it in person, much less a photograph. It was just too big. She felt that maybe if you stared at that view for several weeks straight, your brain might start to comprehend the vastness it was seeing. She drove straight back to Sedona that night.

From Dawn's Journal:

A wonder of nature—the Grand Canyon. How can I comprehend the nature of the universe if I can't even wrap my head around one of earth's natural wonders!

CHAPTER 38

From Dawn's Journal

There are many reasons why my visit to Sedona has been monumental to my life. Since I own an art gallery, it should come as no surprise that art is one of them. I visited the glorious art galleries in town and found myself overwhelmed by the brilliant colors of some of the southwestern artists. It brought out such a longing in me that it was painful. I felt a need for the beauty of the art and the terrain. At one gallery, I stood in front of a painting of a warrior with a flowing cape done in bright oranges, blues, and yellows, and felt tears come to my eyes.

I decided to talk to Judith about painting something for me. I took lots of pictures that day of the art and of the red mountains hoping that they would inspire my artist friend and partner when I got back.

There is something similar in the way I respond to natural beauty and the way I respond to art. They both elevate my mood and open my mind to new ideas. They activate some sort of pleasure center in me and make me want to contemplate the bigger issues of my existence. They are both powerful, positive influences, and I want to spend as much time as possible around them.

CHAPTER 39

Alien Concepts

The next day, Dawn picked up the local newspaper to see what was going on in Sedona. She found a notice about a speaker coming to the St. Andrews Episcopal Church. Camila Fizgerald, a representative of an international UFO contact group, was going to speak on UFO abduction experiences. The talk was being hosted by the Sedona chapter.

Dawn was intrigued. The event was to be held that very night, and she knew she simply had to go. One thing that interested her about the event, aside from the obvious UFO subject, was that it was being presented at an Episcopal church. She couldn't picture any Episcopal churches she had ever attended back home hosting a talk like that. "Only in Sedona" was the phrase that popped into her mind and would continue to do so for her entire trip.

It was Friday night, and the meeting was well attended. About sixty people were there. Dawn walked in and tried to sit near the back in case she wanted to leave early. She ended up sitting next to a tall, handsome man because he was right by the back door and because he was a tall, handsome man. "*Why not?*" she thought with an inner grin, picturing Lola laughing at her.

As she sat, he said hello to her and then said something about there being a lot of people there that night. She agreed and told him that she wished she could talk to everyone in the room because she would bet that every one of them had a great story to tell. The big man squinted his eyes at her and suddenly looked angry. "What are you?" were his exact words. Not "Who are you?" He definitely said, "What."

Dawn looked at him in surprise, but said nothing for a moment. Then she asked warily, "What do you mean?"

"Are you an investigative reporter?" he asked gruffly.

"No, I'm not," she told him, "I just like stories."

He looked at her again, apparently making a decision about her, then relaxed. He said, "Well, then, here's *my* story. Recently I went for a ride to Florida with my star buddy."

"Star buddy?" thought Dawn.

He went on, "My buddy lives in Washington, and the government has got its eye on him, so I can't mention his name. We flew to Florida in his ship."

"Flew in his ship?" thought Dawn.

"And it was great because I'd never been to Florida before. I helped him do some work on the ship there."

The man pulled out some pictures that his star buddy had taken of UFO's and then showed me a picture of some kind of machine. It was shaped like a tiny Taj Mahal. He said, "This is my UFO communications transmitter. It needs adjusting, but I keep it under my bed at night. During the planetary congregation, you could see tiny planets circling over the tip of this baby—like a hologram. It's made of silver and copper and who knows what else. My star buddy gave it to me. When I first got it, it needed lots of adjusting. It gave me terrible headaches for the longest time, but now I sleep well, and I can use it to communicate."

Dawn nodded and smiled and was truly relieved when the speaker was introduced.

Camila Fizgerald claimed to be an UFO abductee and had great sympathy for the numerous people who had similar experiences. She said that there was often no place for people to turn to or talk to about their abduction, so she was happy to be associated with an organization for just that purpose. As such, Camila has heard many stories over the years and seen many "visitation sites." She said that there have been many reports of abduction experiences. For some reason, California, Ohio, and Florida had reported the most abductions in the past year. Camila said that she had seen space ships, Sasquatch footprints, and aliens. She spoke about human experimentation, animal mutilation, and other weird phenomena, all attributed to UFOs.

Camila herself was in her late fifties and while sincere about her topic, she wasn't the best public speaker. She talked in such a rambling-round way that Dawn missed the point of several of her tales because she simply couldn't understand what she said.

In the middle of her talk, Camila played two taped telephone interviews with UFO witnesses. Dawn perked up at this. One had witnessed the same visitation that Camila herself had when she was a teenager. The other witness had been in the Navy, stationed in Roswell, and had seen photos of those famous aliens.

During the talk, the handsome man next to Dawn handed her a book written by Dave W. Chace which depicted drawings of many different kinds of aliens. This was new to her. She had never heard of different types of aliens. She had only heard of the little grey guys with big, slanted eyes.

She mused, *"But I suppose, if they do indeed exist, then why wouldn't there be different types?"* The book showed reptilian-looking aliens, a big hairy Yeti-style creature, and several versions of the little, big-eyed guys. There were even eight-foot tall Nordic blonde women aliens. It was eye-opening to Dawn.

At the end of the talk, Camila introduced the local event organizers. Afterwards, four people stood up and told their stories of personal abduction, including one young man who claimed he had been abducted by a Sasquatch. At that point, the floor was opened to questions from the audience.

The most interesting audience members were two psychologists who had worked with patients who were abductees. They said that their patients felt threatened by the aliens, even long after the abduction.

The patients felt that if they talked about or even remembered the abduction experience, that something terrible would happen to them or their families. A couple of them had to be hospitalized during therapy because, as the memories got closer to consciousness, the patients actually started hemorrhaging. Dawn's heart went out to those people who were in such pain, no matter what was causing it.

Then, the meeting was sort of taken over by people in the audience who wanted to discuss odd things. Several people got up and spoke about autistic children and their theory that the children were related to extra-terrestrials. One of the men said he'd heard that autistic children had a different DNA from the rest of the human race.

*"Where in the world are they getting this idea?"*wondered Dawn.

A woman in the audience talked about a being named Ashtar who was supposed to have come back from the future and was related to the UFOs in some capacity. Dawn perked up again at the familiar name. Ashtar was the name of the being that the channeler had spoken for a couple of nights ago. Dawn thought that was interesting.

The man next to her leaned over again and pointed to the cover of Chace's alien book again. He asked, "You see this?" He pointed to and named each of the aliens on the cover of the book. "They are all under Ashtar's dominion. They are all Dark Allegiance." He said the last part with a clenched fist and nodded at her meaningfully.

"Is that…bad?" she asked.

He looked at her with his eyes wide, "THEY ARE DARK ALLEGIENCE!"

"Whatever that means," thought Dawn. She nodded and smiled to placate the guy, but then, mischievously, she couldn't resist asking him, "So, what are *you?*"

He pulled out a post-it note, wrote something on it, and then he handed it to her. The paper was filled with symbolic writing that could have been runes, or hieroglyphics, for all she knew.

"What does this say?" she asked.

"It says 'Not aligned with Ashtar.'"

"What language is this?" she asked.

"Pleiadian," he nodded, "As in, from the constellation Pleiades."

"Gotcha," she said.

At the end of the meeting, Dawn rose quickly to go so she didn't have to interact with the man any more. Her jury was so far out on him, and it was a relief to get away.

From Dawn's Journal:

As I drove back to the Center tonight, I thought about what I had heard at the meeting. Clearly, there are some odd people involved in all this, but I feel that with so many people reporting such incidents, maybe they shouldn't all be discounted. Something had happened to some of those people, and they had suffered greatly for it. I could feel pain in that room tonight and felt such sympathy for them.

Aside from finding their stories interesting, there is another reason I'm interested in UFOs. Since I've been in Sedona, I've seen that some people, including many channelers of beings from other worlds or dimensions, believe and talk about how those beings are trying to teach people on earth to raise their consciousness so that we can all ascend to higher dimensions. It is my understanding that ascending to higher dimensions brings us closer to God or Source. So I don't want to cut the subject of aliens off if there is a possibility of this being true. Until we all know the truth, it's important to stay open. Not sure if this is a great analogy, but once upon a time, we didn't believe in germs, even when some forward-thinking doctors and scientists tried to educate us about them. When we finally accepted the fact that we all need to wash our hands, especially doctors, it made a world of difference in health care and lowered the mortality rate in hospitals. What I'm saying is, just because we haven't seen something doesn't mean it's not there. So, I'm holding out for proof.

Tonight, when I turned onto the Center's street, I pulled into the parking lot and got out of the car. There are no street lights in that part of Sedona and it was amazingly dark. I felt prickles up and down my spine as I hurried down the driveway to the Center. Just before I closed the front door behind me, I looked up into the star-filled sky and prayed there wouldn't be any big, brightly-lit saucers floating around up there waiting to snatch me up. Honestly, the only alien I want to see is my best friend, Lola, once I get back home.

CHAPTER 40

"Lola, you're just not going to believe this one!" Dawn held her phone and paced excitedly in the back garden of the Center. "Wait, don't tell me. You are enlightened now, and we have to start calling you Guru Dawn of the Light. Or maybe—Dawn of the Dead!" Lola went off into a gale of laughter at her own joke.

"You are such a funny person," said Dawn, drily.

"Actually, I am," said Lola, still chuckling. "But tell me your news." Dawn told her all about the UFO meeting for abductees that she attended the night before.

"Well, you're absolutely right. I don't believe it," said Lola, throwing up her hands in astonished resignation. Unfortunately, she was repotting some geraniums at the time and soil flew everywhere. She sputtered and spit out some loose dirt that had flown into her mouth.

Dawn ignored her yowls and went on, "Oh my God, Lola. I'm not sure I would have believed it either, but once you hear their stories, you can feel it in your heart that these people are telling the truth, as they see it. Something out of this world really happened to them. And, oh my gravy, but I learned a lot about UFOs last night. And, by the way, apparently they're called UAPs now—Unidentified Aerial Phenomena."

"Don't you just hate when people change a perfectly good name that you've known all your life," said Lola, annoyed and combing the dirt out of her hair with her fingers. "Like when Facebook changed to Meta. And Twitter is now just some nonsense name like X! And don't even get me started on the artist formerly known as Prince!"

Dawn chuckled, and Lola went on, "OK, sistah. I've gotta run, but in the meantime, try not to turn into an alien. Not that I could tell, you're so weird anyway."

"Look who's talking. Goodbye, funny lady. I'll beam you up, I mean, I'll call you tomorrow."

CHAPTER 41

From Dawn's Journal

Dammit if I didn't get sick again! I was out in the middle of nowhere, in the desert, hiking. I had to drop my shorts and go to the bathroom behind a rock, very carefully using the spiky, thorny plants as toilet paper, the only thing around except rocks. I felt like an animal, and I hated it. I'd been feeling increasingly sick to my stomach since I'd arrived in Sedona. It didn't feel like a regular little bout of eating something bad or a germ of some kind. My stomach was actually vibrating in my body. I was constantly aware of it. Instinctively, I knew it had something to do with the place itself—Sedona and perhaps the vortices, one of which I happened to be standing on at that moment. The energy from the environment was shaking up my life and literally shaking my insides. I knew I often needed a good shaking up to make me realize things, but this was getting to be ridiculous.

I've heard about how some people can't handle the energy in Sedona and have to leave. I hate the thought that the city was driving me away, but I was getting a little sicker each day and had better face up to it.

I crouched down in the shade of the rocks until I felt a better. Then, I kept hiking.

I headed straight up Cathedral Rock, which is another one of the vortices in Sedona, and took a path which turned out to be kind of a bad choice. Not only was I sick, I was also stuck. I found myself on a steep bluff where I had to make a decision. I could hike down the very steep rock in front of me, or I could circle back the way I had come. The steep way was quick but dangerous; the other way was much longer but a safer walk. The biggest problem was that I was running out of water again, and that was dangerous too. However, if I fell down the steep embankment I might just die of stupidity. Even if I didn't die, I might be laying there awhile, injured with no one around. I was off the main trail. In the end, the water, time, and stupidity won out. I headed down the steep rock, watching every foot placement all the way. It was slippery and scarier than hell. I could hear Lola's voice in my head talking at my funeral, "Yes, dearly beloved, our sistah, Dawn, died of stupidity. I'm surprised it didn't happen a long time ago."

The thought made me giggle as I finally got down to the bottom by holding onto little shrubs and half-sliding, half walking, losing some skin along the way. At the bottom, I looked back up and couldn't believe I had just made it down such a steep drop. It did make me feel like Wonder Woman though. As I started hiking back, my legs felt wobbly in the heat. I assured myself that super heroes often felt that way.

It took a while getting back to the car. Much longer than I'd planned. I keep making this same mistake. I think I have enough water, and I've been wrong every dang time. It's easy to underestimate the amount of water needed. It made me feel dumb and green, but also determined. I had been hiking about three hours with enough water for two. When I finally got back, I gulped down about a ton of water that I had stashed in the car. I was so tired. Thirst does that to you. But I felt powerful, strong, and satisfied with the experience. On my next hike, I would know better. I mean it this time!

CHAPTER 42

The next day found Dawn out hiking again. There is something about the dead quiet in the desert that called to her soul, and she wanted to get as much of it on her trip as possible. Meditating in the desert brought her spirit joy, and she often stopped on the top of a rock to clear her mind and breathe in delightedly.

Coming around a little bluff, she came across a small abandoned house with an old wooden sign on it. The faded, painted lettering said, "The Lone Wolf Annex." The old place gave off memories and lingering elements of sadness, beauty, and grief. A history of humanity. It was the summation of a life, a poem, and Dawn felt it deeply. She had a feeling that she would often think about the Lone Wolf Annex in the future. She thought, *Shoot, I'm turning into a lone wolf. Maybe someday I will hang a sign like that on my house.*

When she got back to the car, she drove out some desert roads and came across an old car graveyard out in the middle of nowhere. Rusted-out shells of several great old cars from the forties, their chrome still somewhat shiny in parts in the glaring sun, lay out among the cactus. It looked like some sort of movie set. Dawn loved graveyards of any kind, but that one was special with its classy old auto-occupants. She made up stories about how the cars got to be there. She sat on one old fender and drank a beer from a cooler in her van, watching a rainstorm in the distance. It was a magical afternoon.

When she got back to the Light Center, she pulled into the yard, and there were some other cars parked beside hers. The trunk of one of them was open, and there was a young man rummaging around in it. She had seen him briefly before in the Center when she was talking to Erich and Krysta. He was somewhere in his late twenties with long, dark wavy hair, dark eyebrows, and piercing eyes. His name was John. He turned and asked Dawn her name, then he asked her to sit down on his blanket with him for a minute by his car. He said he felt like just being with her. It was a little unnerving to Dawn at first, sitting on a blanket with a stranger, and a young, gorgeous one at that, but she found his confidence magnetizing. So she thought, "*What the heck,*" and took a moment to sit with him. On the blanket, they sat cross-legged, facing each other, and he reached over and held her hand without saying a word. He looked into her eyes, and she held his look. Dawn only took about five minutes to sit with him, then thanked him and left. She was grateful to him for his sharing.

From Dawn's Journal:

My whole trip seems like it was filled with these sort of fast, ten-minute-long, weird interludes with unusual people and situations, each one more interesting than the last. This one was just a momentary encounter, but it felt like a blessing.

CHAPTER 43

"So, you'll be home tomorrow, right? I can't wait to see you," said Lola, excitedly.

"Yes, my flight leaves in the afternoon. Maybe we can all meet at the gallery for coffee the next morning?"

"Great, I'll tell everyone."

"OK, I hate to say goodbye to Sedona in some ways, Lola. It's changed me."

"Maybe you'd better wear a name tag when I pick you up from the airport. I might not recognize you."

"Ha ha. Boy, I've missed that awesome wit," said Dawn, sarcastically but with a smile in her voice.

"Do you think I don't know that? Now get on that plane and come home. Love you, sistah."

"Love you back. See you soon!"

CHAPTER 44

There were a couple of things Dawn wanted to do before she left. She wanted to visit the big medicine wheel at the Airport vortex that night, and she also wanted to visit the Holy Cross Chapel first thing in the morning.

That evening after dinner, she hiked up to the big medicine wheel and performed a ceremony as the sun went down. She prayed in the center of the wheel and asked God to use her for his will. It felt powerful and beautiful. She thought of her sistahs back home, Lola, Bea, Judith, and Helen, and asked blessings for them. She hoped that they could help her sort out the things that she had been learning on her trip when she got back home. She thought of her children holding down the fort with the family business and doing such a great job. Then, she realized that her thoughts of her family and friends were the gift of the medicine wheel that night.

From Dawn's Journal:

So often when I pray, I am amazed when God's answers come immediately. It felt very similar to what was happening with my visions since I arrived in Sedona. I realized that I could control the visions now to the extent that I could make a vision appear at will and ask for a message from it. It works like this: I would sit down, ask for a vision, go into myself. The vision pops up, message is received, BAM, it's done—go home. Very time saving. This had been a huge awakening for me. If I learned nothing else from my journey, that alone would be plenty enough.

My prayers work the same way sometimes, except they were more of a knowing rather than a visual revelation. I know they are all gifts, and I feel so grateful and close to God tonight.

CHAPTER 45

The next morning, Dawn said her goodbyes and was having a difficult time of it. She had made fast friends with some of the people, especially Naomi, Erich, and Krysta, and was sad to leave them. She hugged them all and promised to stay in touch. Then she got in her car, waving out the window as she drove away.

On her way out of town she visited the Chapel of the Holy Cross which is a beautiful Roman Catholic chapel built in 1956 right into the red rock buttes of Sedona within the Coconino National Forest. Many people believe the chapel is a vortex itself because the energy is so powerful there, it is easy to feel overwhelmed inside. Dawn sat on a pew in the chapel, listening to glorious music and felt like she might cry. She could feel the love of God and the good energy there, even when the place was crawling with tourists. She could tell that they felt it too. That's why they come here. It draws them, and it's a shared experience.

As she drove out of town, the red rocks never looked more beautiful and she dared anyone to come to Sedona and not have some sort of spiritual experience. It is some of God's best work.

She got on the highway and headed north. She felt satisfied and that she had done what she had come to do. It was time to go home.

From Dawn's Journal

The lessons of Sedona had an immediate impact on my life.

1. I learned to be cautious but open to people and experiences. There was a lot of knowledge to learn from them and a lot of love to receive from them too. No matter what the people I met believed in, they were just further proof to me that everyone is seeking God in one way or the other.

2. I learned to call upon and ask for visions, not only for myself, but for others as well. This was an amazing revelation to me. It meant that I could use the visions at will to help me and others with answers to the oh-so-many questions we have in our lives. It meant that I could use the visions when I needed them. It had taken me over sixty years to discover this. I am obviously a slow learner. Apparently, I needed to take a remedial course in Psychic 101 studies. That's what happens when you don't explore your gifts. I talked about them on this trip, and I learned so much. Sedona was like a giant classroom for me. I felt that I would come back one day and learn more.

3. I also learned that I was supposed to use my gifts to help others, that this would be my work for the rest of my life. That was the most exciting lesson of all. I don't know how I will do that yet. But I will do it somehow. I know I will.

4. I learned that kindness and service to others goes a long way in opening up a heart and raising consciousness.

5. Everything I saw and learned on my trip was fascinating. But out of everything that claimed to raise my frequency and consciousness, I'm going to focus on meditation and being of service to others.

Now I have the exciting but daunting task of living the rest of my life with these lessons. I believe there is immense joy coming my way.

CHAPTER 46

Dawn was sipping coffee and holding up her her phone so the Sistahs could see her many Sedona photos. "OK, Judith, take a look at this picture. This one is of Bell Rock."

Judith took the phone and studied it before showing it around the table to Bea, Helen, and Lola.

"This is just so gorgeous," said Helen.

"I love the way you caught the sunset colors too," said Judith.

"Just stunning," agreed Bea.

"So do you think you can paint it for me?' asked Dawn.

Judith looked again at the photo and said, "I'd be happy to give it a try. I'd really enjoy doing it since it's so special to you."

Dawn went on, "I saw so much beautiful Sedona art with colorful skies and mountains. I was tempted to buy one there, but it seemed silly when I own a gallery, and I am best friends with a fantastic artist. I'd rather you paint it. It would mean more to me."

"You have a birthday coming up, partner. It saves me from having to think of a gift for you."

"I can't wait. It will be such a beautiful reminder of my trip," said Dawn, helping herself to another of Helen's scones. "Let's hold a medicine wheel ceremony before you start the painting so it will be blessed."

"Do we have a medicine wheel?" asked Judith.

Dawn swallowed a bite of scone and answered nonchalantly, "I'm going to build one in Lola's backyard."

Judith looked over at Lola, "Does Lola know that?"

Lola rolled her eyes, then chuckled. "She does now!"

"OK, I want to let y'all know that I'm going to start doing tarot readings once a week at the gallery. I think I'm ready. And of course I will always read for any of you anytime and for free."

"I'm first!" yelled Lola. "And there had better be a get-rich card in that deck, preferably with a winning lottery ticket attached to it!"

Dawn went on, "And also I want to invite every one of you to come to the first meditation group next week, right here at the gallery. We're going to advertise it to the public and do one every week on Wednesday nights. Isn't that exciting? It will be our local contribution to helping people see how we are all connected and to raise our vibrations. We'll start with the class and see where the momentum takes us." "We're in," said Bea, looking around for confirmation. "We're so impressed with how much joy your journey has brought you, dear. I believe in group prayer, and I think it might be like group meditation. I've heard that with prayer you're talking to God, but with meditation God is talking to you. We're communicating with God in one shape or another."

"Bea's right," said Helen. "And I'll be happy to lead some of the meditations. I've done it before at some of my Reiki conferences."

"Oh thank God. I was hoping you'd volunteer, Helen," laughed Dawn. "I'm going to need some help. It's all so new, but I believe in it so much."

"Do you think Lynn might come?" asked Judith.

Dawn hesitated, "You mean—come here? To the meditation group?"

Judith went on excitedly, "Sure. She might even be interested in leading a meditation some time."

Dawn stole a look at Lola and said nothing. But Bea, sharp as ever, saw their exchange, and she narrowed her eyes and asked, "Wait a minute. You're not still emailing Lynn pretending to be Dan, are you, Dawn?"

Dawn tried to look innocent and fiddled with her coffee cup. Lola went diving into her purse pretending to look for something.

"You are, aren't you!" Bea shook her head in disgust. "Oh Dawn, how could you?"

"Bea, you don't understand. I still don't know if she and Dan had a thing going. It's been crazy-hard getting it out of her. And I have to know. I keep hoping she'll slip up and say something in an email."

"Dear, you're going to have to ask her straight out. That's all there is to it. This isn't right, and it could drag on forever. If you want to know the truth, you have to ask."

"I can't now, Bea. It's gone too far. It will just be too embarrassing at this point."

"Oh, it's gone too far alright," said Helen, rolling her eyes.

Dawn asked hopefully, "Will you do it for me, Bea?"

"No, dear, I won't," said Bea, shaking her head. "This is something only you can do."

Dawn groaned.

Bea went on, "But you don't have to do it alone. That what your sistahs are for." She winked at Dawn.

Dawn looked from one sistah to another. "You'll be there to back me up?"

"Of course we will. We'll be right there with you when you confront Lynn. You can do it at the meditation group next week if Lynn agrees to come."

"Oh thank you so much, sistahs!" gushed Dawn. "It's such a tricky situation. Ironically, I really like Lynn. I'm starting to consider her a friend, and I would hate to lose her at this point. I'm going to need my sistahs."

"Yep, you've stepped in it deep this time, Dawn," said Judith nodding. "But don't worry, we'll pull you out. But you know, it occurs to me that in your new spiritual quest, you are learning to forgive and extend love. That's not really irony. That's progress!"

CHAPTER 47

Later that day, Dawn texted Lynn:

> *Lynn, there's three things I need to tell you.*
>
> *First, thank you so much for sending me to Sedona. It was the trip of a lifetime, and I can wait to talk to you about it!*
>
> *Second, Please, please, please come to our first meditation class next Wednesday night at the Gumbeaux Sistahs gallery in Covington at 6pm. I'm so looking forward to the Sistahs meeting you. They are going to love you*
>
> *And third…this is the hard part. I have something to tell you that may shock you. I hate to sound dramatic, but I want to prepare you a little. It's time for me to be honest. I'll tell you at the class. Come a little early so we'll have time together to talk.*
>
> *OK, that's it. See you next week. (Please come!)*

CHAPTER 48

"I asked Lynn to come early, so she ought to be here any minute," explained Dawn to the five sistahs as they set up a circle of chairs in the gallery for the meditation class. Helen was planning to do a guided meditation for the night, and she'd also brought her famous scones for afterwards. Lola was setting up the coffee pot.

"Are you ready for this, dear?" asked Bea, glancing worriedly at Dawn.

"Oh, hell no, Bea. I'm expecting this to be so awkward. But at this point, I just have to bite the bullet and get it done."

While Helen was readying her meditation music, Judith looked up at the front window in time to see a shadow pass and said, "Oh dear, Dawn. I think this is Lynn now."

The front door opened, and Lynn stuck her head in and yelled, "Are there any Gumbeaux Sistahs in here?" Her hearty laugh filled the gallery.

"Come in, come in," said Dawn, smiling nervously. "Come meet the Sistahs. Everyone, this is Lynn."

Lynn stepped inside in her flowing skirt and bangle bracelets that clinked while she walked. Bea reached out her hand and took Lynn's warmly in hers. "Hi Lynn. I'm Bea. Dawn has told us so much about you."

To which Lola added with a smirk, "Yes, more than you'd ever dream." She stifled a giggle when Dawn shot her a warning look.

"We couldn't wait to meet you," added Helen.

Dawn introduced Lynn to each sistah, and afterwards Lynn said with a mischievous grin, "And I'm Lynn, Dawn's crazy psychic friend."

"Come have some coffee and sit down," said Dawn with a slight quaver to her voice.

Lynn looked hard at Dawn and asked, "Dawn are you OK? You look, I don't know, upset? Anxious?"

"With good reason," murmured Lola, rolling her eyes.

"Don't pay her any mind, Lynn," said Dawn, sitting down next to her. "I mean, the truth is—no, I'm not alright, and I am very anxious. I have something to tell you."

"Is that right…" said Lynn, slowly. She fixed a steely gaze directly at Dawn. "Is it something important? Something serious?"

"I'm afraid so," answered Dawn, wringing her hands together.

"Something that you should have mentioned a long time ago, perhaps?"

Dawn hesitated, "Well, yes…"

"Something like—you have been emailing me pretending to be Dan? That you are, in fact, Dan's widow, and that my old friend Dan is deceased?"

Dawn gasped along with the rest of the Sistahs.

"Oh my gravy," said Dawn loudly, slapping her forehead with her palm. "You knew? How long have you known? How did you figure it out?"

"I've known for weeks, Dawn. Ever since you first walked through my door for a reading. Although I suspected before that. Ever since your first email to me as Dan. You signed off as 'Sincerely, Dan.' I mean, that was so weird. I know it's been awhile, but Dan didn't talk that way. Nobody does—at least not to me. So, I got suspicious, and I googled him. Then I found out on Facebook that he had passed, and by the way—I'm really so sorry for your loss, Dawn. Dan was a wonderful man. I saw on his funeral home website that he was survived by you and your two children. So, I searched for you on Facebook, and there you were in all your photos. I suspected it might be you who was emailing, but I knew for sure when you walked in my door."

"But why didn't you say something," asked Dawn, mortified.

"A couple of reasons. First, I was curious about why you'd pretend to be Dan, and second, I'm a bit of a stinker and decided that two could play at the deception game."

"Oh my gravy, Lynn! You *are* a stinker!"

"As I like to say, I'm that and so much more. The question that remains, however, is why you would pretend to be Dan. What was all that for? I kept expecting you to stop once we started to become friends, but nope. You just kept it up. So," she shrugged, "I did too."

"We *are* starting to be friends, Lynn, and it's become important to me. And that's why I'm telling you the truth today. But why I did it is not the only remaining question. I can't stand it, and I have to know—what was your relationship to Dan? Were you lovers? Did he have feelings for you? We were married when he went on that trip with you. We were separated but still legally married and talking about getting back together. And he never once mentioned you. He did mention a trip to California, but never said he wasn't alone. This has been killing me. I honestly thought if I emailed you back after you first wrote Dan, you might say something in an email that would give me a clue. But you never did! So, I need to know. Who were you to my husband, Lynn?" Tears formed in her eyes as she looked at the other women, waiting to finally learn the truth.

Lynn's eyes watered up as well, and she looked with great sympathy at her new friend, "I thought it might be something like this. And now I'm sorry for continuing the charade. I just thought at first that you were a meddling case trying to get gossip. That's why I rushed you during our meetings, so you wouldn't have time to get in your Dan questions. But now that I know you, I realize how much pain it might have caused you."

"Oh dear Lord!" cried Dawn. "I'm the one who should be sorry."

"But Dawn, you had nothing to worry about with Dan and I. Yes, we did take a couple of fabulous trips together, but we weren't the only ones there. There was a group of us that went on a spiritual adventure website and found each other. Several of us took some life-changing trips together. I was especially fond of a couple of the people in the group, and Dan was one of them. When I was going back to revisit the places we'd stopped at, I emailed a couple of them—not just Dan, by the way. I just wanted to remind them of that amazing time."

"So, you weren't romantically involved with him?" pressed Dawn.

"No. Mind you, I thought he was gorgeous, and I'll admit to a bit of attraction to him, but that was never going to happen. I've never seen a man so in love. He talked about you all the time. And besides, that group of friends was sharing something that changed our lives. It bonded us all in a different way."

"It sounds like the kind of relationship you had with Erich in Sedona, Dawn. Kind of a brother in your shared experiences. See, I told you that you had nothing to worry about, with Lynn," Lola crowed.

"You said no such thing!" scolded Dawn. Then to Lynn she said, "Good Lord, I'm so sorry. I've been such an ass. Can you forgive me?"

"Dawn, I'm glad you did it. Look where it brought you. You ended up making your own spiritual journey because of all this."

"Whew, I'm glad we got all the truth out at last, dears," added Bea.

"Well, not quite all of the truth," said Lynn with a sudden, unexpected sadness.

"What else could there be?" asked Helen.

She turned to Dawn. "Remember when I told you that I got a new tattoo on my stomach? Well, I didn't tell you what it was."

"I wasn't sure it was my business to ask back then," said Dawn.

"If we're going to be friends, then I think you should know. In fact, I'll show you."

Before anyone could protest, Lynn lifted up her loose-fitting blouse and revealed a tattoo printed in big block letters across her middle. It read: DO NOT RESUSITATE.

The Sistahs gawked, and Dawn actually gasped and asked, "Good lord, Lynn. What is that? What does this mean?"

Lynn looked at her friend and shrugged. "It's not good, girls. I've been battling breast cancer for the last couple of years. I've had a double mastectomy, and it's been a hell of a fight, let me tell you."

"Oh no!" cried Dawn and the Sistahs looked at each other in shock.

"I'm afraid so. And listen I have to just say it. I'm pretty sure that I don't have a lot more time to go, and I am running out of energy. But I didn't want to go out and have the doctors bring me back again and again to just keep going through it all. When my time comes, I want to go and stay gone. I know we don't really die, that we go on in some other capacity. We're energetic beings, and scientists tell us that you can't destroy energy. You can only transform it. I'm actually hoping to come back as Nicole Kidman." She cackled with laughter, and the Sistahs couldn't help but chuckle at that.

"Dawn's coming back as a porcupine because she's so prickly," said Lola, grinning.

"And Lola will be a slug—for obvious reasons," retorted Dawn.

The Sistahs dissolved into laughter. Lynn wiped her eyes and looked around, saying, "Whew! I'm glad I came. I needed this! At any rate, I guess I wanted to tell you and your friends about this because, well, I don't want to be a burden, but I actually would like to have friends when I die. I've kind of let that part of my life go. The friends part. Some of my friends have passed and others I've just lost touch with over the years. It sure seems like a mistake now. Seriously, girls, I could use some friends."

Dawn looked at her new friend, then threw her arms around Lynn.

The other sistahs reached out to hug her too and Bea spoke up through her tears, "Boy, did you come to the right place, Lynn. We would love to have you as our new sistah!"

"You have no idea what that means to me. Thank you. Thank you so much."

Lola couldn't help but break in with some comic relief, "Lynn, we'll make you so sick of us. As a matter of fact, you might want to rethink all this. We're nauseatingly affectionate—as you can see."

"I'm rethinking nothing," said Lynn firmly. "A deal's a deal." She smiled.

"You got it, sistah," smiled Dawn.

"C'mon now everybody," said Helen, wiping her eyes. "We have a dozen people coming here any second for meditation class."

"She's right. Let's talk afterwards. Lynn, I want to know all about everything. But first, help me finish getting these chairs out," said Dawn anxiously.

As Bea grabbed a folding chair, she told Lynn, "This is going to be such a great group. Helen is so good at these guided meditations."

"That's right," said Judith. "Everyone is excited about tonight. And in the future, we thought we might try different things like Toning, or even trying to contact a UFO!"

"Maybe we can talk them into abducting Dawn," laughed Lola.

CHAPTER 49

Two days later Dawn checked in with Sondraya on the phone.

"So good to hear your voice again, Dawn. Sedona misses you!"

"No doubt I'll be back again one of these days. Sedona stays with you, doesn't it?"

"That it does. So, what did you want to talk about today? I pulled your astrological chart for our phone call today."

"I just wanted to check in with you because I feel like I'm growing a little more confident in the work I'm supposed to be doing now. I'm meditating and doing some readings for some friends and others, and the more I do it, the more right it feels. Can you tell me anything that will help me at this stage?"

"What I'm seeing for you is very exciting, Dawn. You need to be ready for what comes your way because the universe is knocking at your door right now. You are on the part of your journey that is about mastery and completion.

"You have a lot of water in your chart—you pick up too much energy from others and need to recover. You need alone time. But you are going to have to deal with that because you're needed now in the world.

"You are in the first years of psychic maturity. It's already started, but it's an expansion cycle. You are exploring, and you need to act on it. Identity can shift from ego to soul. It's time to look beyond humanness and into your divine, angelic, galactic self. It's a great awakening time for you and many others.

"Uranus is in the heavens directly overhead. It's a major turning point. Dreams come true now. Do not be afraid and dive in. There is healing around you. Our minds are magical—use them to command and demand. Ask God to clear out doubt about your purpose. Love yourself. Ask God to help you love yourself like He loves you. We are divine, angelic beings. Believe in yourself. Identify with divinity. Ask God to show you how to believe in yourself."

"I keep praying and meditating, Sondraya. I'm trying to be positive and confident going forward," Dawn told her.

"The Finger of God keeps showing up in your chart. In fact, Dawn, I've never seen so many references to it in a reading. Be in constant, inner conversation with God. There is mystical, magical potential here. Neptune is present and is the most spiritual planet. It's a sign of total rebirth. All you have to do is be willing.

"Do everything you can to further your relationships with God. Talk to him like He is your best friend. Now is the mystical time—a great awakening, cosmic consciousness. What do you want, Dawn? You need to get as detailed and particular as you can be and say out loud, 'I want!' You need to command and demand."

Dawn nodded, "I really feel drawn to helping people right now. I'm not quite sure how to put it all into play."

"Take some small action step towards what you would like to do. Any action will do. You've started doing readings and visions for your friends. Now ask them to spread the word for you so you can get more practice. Don't worry about being perfect. Part of being perfect is being imperfect. The way will open to you as you go along. Ask for energy and enthusiasm. You can go deeper than you think. And don't forget to keep a journal.

"We all came here to have this human experience. Any kind of healing you need, believe in it.

This year is full of opportunities. There will be all kinds of leads and connections. Your life will not necessarily be easy, but that gives you mastery. Go into action. In mastery, you'll be getting back to peace and gratitude. It's time to learn."

"I'm anxious to learn," said Dawn. "I'm reading and talking to people, trying to gather as much information as I can. I think I just need practice."

"Don't be afraid to go big," Sondraya continued. "Sometimes people can't handle that, but you can. Your best friend is God! He puts people and angels in your life that are here for a reason. To test you. To love you. Find your people. Find them with a magical mind set. Stay open."

"By the way, the crows are no longer following me," reported Dawn.

"I figured they would move on. I'm sure they left to tell someone else that it was time for them to draw close to Spirit. That's the way of it. Dawn, my friend, just know that this is your time. Jupiter wants to give you what you want. Envision it—and you can have it. Command and demand. Attract it. It's yours for the asking."

CHAPTER 50

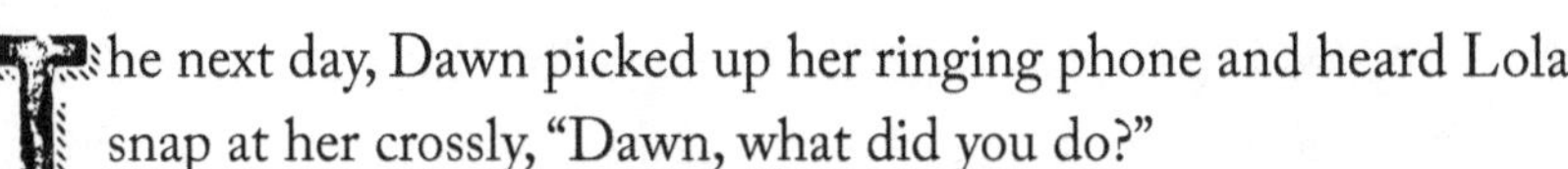

The next day, Dawn picked up her ringing phone and heard Lola snap at her crossly, "Dawn, what did you do?"

"What are you talking about? I didn't do anything. I don't think," answered Dawn, confused.

"Don't even try to tell me that you didn't send all these birds over to my house!"

"What birds?"

"My backyard is full of crows!" wailed Lola.

Dawn almost dropped the phone she was laughing so hard.

CHAPTER 51

"Good gravy, Dawn," said Lola, yelling into the phone. "I've never seen such red mountains. Sedona is mind-blowing!"

Dawn laughed at her friend's exuberance. "I knew you'd love it, sistah. So what's on the agenda today?"

"I'm going to Bell Rock, then visiting the Holy Cross Chapel, then on to the Buddhist Stupa. And, of course, I have an appointment with Sondraya."

"I'm totally jealous, Lola. I want to do it all over again. Tell me what she says, OK? I'm so excited for you."

"How was the meditation group last night?" asked Lola.

"The group is growing already. We had to bring in extra chairs last night. People can feel the spirit and energy of the group. It's powerful."

"Well, I'm looking forward to checking in when I get home. But listen, there's someone here who want to say something to you. Hang on."

Dawn could hear the phone being handed off, and a new voice came on, "Hello there!" said Lynn's familiar, joyful voice.

"Hello yourself, sistah," said Dawn, delighted. "How are you holding up?"

"I'm hanging in there but taking it slowly. Lola does the hiking, and I do the part where I sit in the foothills and meditate. It works out."

Dawn asked, "And how is Sedona taking to Lola?"

Dawn could hear the smile in her voice as Lynn said, "Everyone here at the Center loves her, of course. She's such a smart-ass. But I can tell that the experience is blowing her away."

Dawn shook her head with a smile, "That's Lola, alright."

Lynn covered her hand over the phone and lowered her voice. "Dawn, there's something I need to tell you. I just need to say this to you today. You know that this might be my last trip, right?"

Dawn listened quietly with a stab in her heart for her new friend. She choked out a mumbled, "I know, Lynn."

"So, I just want to thank you for suggesting that Lola and I make this trip together. I know it was an iffy deal with my health issues, but it's been a miracle for my frame of mind."

"No problem, Lynn. Besides, someone's got to keep Lola out of trouble."

Lynn went on, "And thank you for making me a Gumbeaux Sistah and calling me your friend. It's one of the honors of my life."

Dawn held back threatening tears but broke out in a grin, "Gumbeaux on, sistah."

"Same to you, Crow Woman."

From Dawn's Journal:

Even though I'm back from my trip, my spiritual journey is just beginning. It's hard for me to explain how much happiness and excitement has entered my life since this all began. I have faith that my journey will continue and be a joyous one—and hopefully involve a lot less crow poop!

CHAPTER 52

Phone Home

Dawn nestled into her comfy couch with a glass of merlot and picked up the receiver of her old pink landline phone sitting in her lap. The marvelous thing about this phone was that, while it was a land line, it wasn't landed or attached to any line. Nor was it bluetooth connected. It was just an old phone that she used for a very specific purpose. She used it when she wanted or needed to "talk" to the spirit of her deceased husband, Dan, as she did now.

Taking a sip of the wine, she pushed buttons on the phone. She didn't keep track of how many buttons she pushed or which specific order she pushed them. She just pushed and then waited, just in case this was the day that Dan would actually pick up and say hello. She sighed and then launched right into what she needed to get off her chest.

"Dan, I'm so glad I don't have to kick your ass. I can't tell you what a relief it was to find out that you weren't fooling around with Lynn while we were married. That would not have been pretty, husband of mine. I probably would have had you exhumed and re-buried in the middle of the Mojave in an unmarked grave!" She laughed and knew that if Dan were with her, he would be laughing with her.

"Still, I don't know why you didn't talk to me about your spiritual trip with her. If you were here, I'd be talking your ears off about mine. What an amazing experience for both of us, I'm sure. I feel as if it would have strengthened our bond. But, oh well. I was thinking about it and figured out you didn't say anything because we are both from conservative backgrounds and we went to church every Sunday. Maybe you thought you were going against the church or something. Well, guess what, old man, I have news for you. I still go to church sometimes. I love our church family, and that is a wonderful place to be still and feel close to God. So yes, I'm still in our pew on Sunday mornings. I just think there's things we don't know, and I think the wonders of the universe are all good news, and I'd like to know more about them."

She shook her head with regret. "But listen, dear husband, I still want to talk to you and when it's my time to go, I'll expect you to be there at that end of that tunnel, front and center. We'll get us a big bucket of fried chicken, some wine and cheesecake (there's no calories after death, right), and have us a heavenly picnic and talk for hours. And man, what a talk that will be, won't it? Hopefully, you'll have some juicy universal secrets to share."

She smiled into the phone, "In the meantime, please say hello to everyone and give Spirit a giant hug for me, if that's possible. And I'll ask the angels to take the best care of you too. Hang tight, Dan. Be happy. And if you can, keep the crows out of my garden, alright? I'll be with you soon enough, my love. OK. Well that's it. Bye for now, and I'll call you again soon."

She hung up the phone, but not before kissing it mightily, with a clear head and a full heart.

The End

JAX'S NOTE

n case you haven't guessed it, Dawn's journey was based on my own first spiritual journey back in 1993. Back then, I yearned to make such a journey because I felt that strong, existential pull that haunts us all eventually. I knew in my heart there was more out there to learn, and I didn't know how to find it. I also felt strongly that I needed to physically go out into the world and search for it and not just read about it in a book. It was all very new to me, but it felt correct and necessary. The roadblock was that I didn't have the money back then to take an actual trip. However, I had an old, gold Rolex watch given to me by an ex-boyfriend. Once I made up my mind that I needed to go…I never sold anything so fast in my life! And then I was off.

I followed advice from trusted friends, and I also read a book called *Sanctuaries* by Jack and Marcia Kelly to help me find spiritual spots to visit. That book is still available, but since that kind of book is hard to keep current, some of the information on the places in the book might be outdated. So, if you use it, double check the info before you head out. Also note, that I changed the names of many places and people I visited for everyone's privacy.

The reason I wanted to write about my journey is because that trip had such a profound effect on my life. It inspired me to pursue a spiritual practice, art, and writing—whole new worlds for me.

I learned so much on my trip about raising my frequencies and consciousness that, at first, it was hard to discern what my life's spiritual practice should be. But after studying, and trial and error, my journey has since allowed me to focus my practice on meditation, kindness and service to others, and creating art that promotes love and awareness. You will find your own way too. It's worth the trip and it is the reason I recommend making a spiritual journey to everyone, even if you do it from home.

One thing I didn't state outright in the book is how much fun I had on my journey. What a blast!

Note that I added some tips on how to start your journey elsewhere in this book. Just be sure to be cautious and use your intuition, trusted referrals, research, and smarts to keep yourself safe. Not everyone is out for your best interest, but luckily, most people are.

Going on an actual, physical journey has the advantage of offering personal experiences which shake up the brain and refresh the heart. But if you do the journey from home, you can enjoy the new experience of meeting teachers and like-minded people closer geographically to you. Both are never-ending journeys of which I never tire.

Look for your teachers and your people. Trust your intuition. Find your bliss.

Having said all this, I recognize that we are all on a spiritual journey right now, whether we recognize it or not and like it or not. We all find our own way, and it's so worth the trip.

Bon voyage, sistahs!
Jax

RECIPES

Monk's Bread

3-1/2 c. wheat flour
4 tsp baking powder
2 tsp salt
½ cup oil
½ cup honey
¾ cup hot water or warm milk

Directions:

1. Sift dry ingredients. Add honey to hot water (or milk). Mix oil and honeyed water together.
2. Pour oil and honeyed water into dry ingredients and mix. Makes smooth soft dough (not sticky). Knead.
3. Roll out to 3/16" and cut it into small rounds or shapes (cross, butterfly, heart, etc).
4. Place on parchment paper covered baking sheet.
5. Bake at 400 degrees for 10 to 15 minutes. Cool on racks. It smells heavenly!

Chicken Etouffee

Ready In: 1hr 15mins. Serves 14

1 cup flour

1 cup butter

4 cups onions, chopped

2 cups celery, chopped

2 cups bell peppers, chopped

3 tablespoons of your favorite Cajun seasoning

2 cups chicken stock

2 lbs. chicken, thigh meat, cooked and chopped

4 cups long grain white rice, dry

2 bay leaves

2 garlic cloves, chopped

1/2 cup green onion, chopped

2 tablespoons parsley, chopped

Directions:

Cook rice as directed .While rice is cooking, start your dark roux. In a sauté pan, melt the butter over medium heat, add flour, and whisk continuously for about 15-20 minutes until color is a medium-dark brown, a little darker than peanut butter, and should smell very 'nutty'. Time may vary; it's more about the color and smell. Add the roux to a cold stock pot to stop the cooking. Add the Cajun seasoning to your roux, along with the onions, celery, and peppers. Turn heat to low-medium and stir until well blended and simmering. Add chicken, fresh garlic, and half of the chicken stock to the pot, and stir. While stirring, gradually add more stock until the desired thickness is reached. Add bay leaves, and cook for 30 minutes over medium heat. Add green onion and parsley, stir, then serve over cooked rice.

New Orleans Pralines

Makes 15 to 20 pralines
1 cup granulated sugar
1 cup packed brown sugar
1/2 cup evaporated milk
4 tablespoons unsalted butter, cubed
2 teaspoons pure vanilla extract
1 1/2 cups toasted and coarsely chopped pecans
1/4 cup boiling water, if needed

Directions:

1. Prepare a baking sheet by lining it with aluminum foil and spraying the foil with nonstick cooking spray. Alternatively, you can use a silicone mat or parchment paper on top of the baking sheet. Do not use wax paper, it will melt.
2. In a medium saucepan over medium heat, combine the white sugar, brown sugar, and evaporated milk.
3. Stir until the sugar dissolves. Once all is well mixed, insert a candy thermometer. Cook the candy, stirring occasionally, until the thermometer reads 240 F.
4. Once the proper temperature is reached, remove the pan from the heat and drop the cubes of butter on top, without stirring. Allow the sugar mixture to sit for 1 minute.
5. Add the vanilla extract and pecans.
6. Begin to stir smoothly and constantly with a wooden spoon; the candy will begin to thicken and appear lighter in color. Continue to stir until the candy starts to hold its shape. It should still be easy to stir, but don't overdo it, as pralines quickly go from fluid to rock-solid.
7. Once the confection has a lighter opaque-brown color and is holding its shape, work quickly and drop small spoonfuls of the candy onto the prepared baking sheet. Because the

pralines will start to set in the saucepan, you need to spoon out the candy as fast as you safely can. If the candy stiffens before you're done scooping, add a spoonful of boiling hot water and stir until it loosens, then continue scooping until you have formed all the pralines.

8.   Allow the candy to fully set at room temperature; it should take about 30 minutes for the pralines to harden. Store the pralines in an airtight container at room temperature. Enjoy!

HOW TO TAKE
A SPIRITUAL JOURNEY
(EVEN IF YOU DO IT FROM HOME)

"The breeze at dawn has secrets to tell you. Don't go back to sleep. You must ask for what you really want. Don't go back to sleep. People are going back and forth across the doorsill where the two worlds touch. The door is round and open. Don't go back to sleep."

–Rumi

What is a Spiritual Journey?

A spiritual journey is a personal quest we undertake to reconnect with Spirit, release attachment to the ego, and rediscover our true nature. In a nutshell, the spiritual journey is about returning to the Center of our being. Listening to the Soul's call to reunite with Spirit is our deepest longing and highest calling as a species, sometimes called Enlightenment.

Here are 7 signs you're being called to take a spiritual journey:

1. You feel that something is missing in your life.
2. You sense that there's *much more* **to life than meets the eye**.
3. You're experiencing strange synchronicities, signs, or omens.

4. You're shedding your old self, and you are transforming, but you don't know who you truly are yet.
5. You experience bouts of melancholy, depression, and existential crisis.
6. You feel extra sensitive and fragile.
7. A lot of what you once valued seems meaningless and empty.

Getting in touch with our soul is the process of opening to our true nature. Examples of soul work practices include *self-inquiry, prayer, contemplation, meditation, mirror work,* and anything that involves cultivating a sense of *being*.

Five different parts of the spiritual journey are as follows:

1. Hearing the Call and beginning to explore consciousness
2. Awakening to fresh possibilities and renewed hope
3. Facing our demons and healing our traumas
4. Rebirth & heart openings
5. Illumination & integrating its aspects into our daily lives

The above five phases are by no means linear or static—they are cyclical and ever-deepening.

How to Begin Your Spiritual Journey (7 Steps)

Everyone's spiritual journey is unique, ever-changing, and ongoing.

If you wish to find truth, peace, profound love, deep freedom, and your ultimate home, beginning your spiritual journey is not only important but *crucial.*

Understandably, you might feel a bit intimidated and lost, not knowing where to start. So here are some tips:

1. Be open to the people and experiences you encounter, but be careful. Trust your intuition.
2. Be gentle and go at your own pace so you don't get overwhelmed. Go gently, but deeply in your learning.
3. Tune into the deepest yearning of your heart, your *holy longing.*

Listen to your heart. One of the best ways to do this is to place a soft hand over your heart, let all thoughts go, and drop into a sense of stillness. Then ask yourself, "What is it that I truly, *deeply* **yearn for, above all else?"**

Finding your holy longing will provide you with the *fuel and compass* to direct your spiritual search. Instead of being outwardly led by the egoist self, you'll be inwardly led by the heart and soul. You may even find that as you progress through your spiritual journey that your holy longing will evolve and mature.

4. Pay attention to philosophies, tools, or practices that intrigue you

Once you've figured out your *holy longing,* simply pay attention. Notice what spiritual fields, ideas, philosophies, and practices call to you that relate to your deepest calling. Walk a path with heart. This is the path you're *meant* to be on.

5. Go deep-diving

Jumping from practice to practice can be useful *at the beginning* (to become familiar with the territory). But if we get into the addictive habit of finding the "next and best" spiritual practice, tool, workshop, etc, we are doing ourselves a great disservice. We are not only approaching spirituality with a materialistic mindset, but we're also avoiding the fundamental purpose of the spiritual path: to discover our True Nature.

Once you've done some dabbling here and there (this might involve reading books, watching YouTube videos, Gaia.com, attending lectures and workshops, etc.) it's time to slow down and commit to something. Don't worry if you discover later down the road that the path you're on is not for you, *you can always change route.*

What paths, practices, and teachings speak to you on a profound level? What has benefited you the most? Begin to circle around that topic, practice, or path and dedicate your full attention to it.

6.   Record what you've learned and experienced

One of the simplest ways of recording what you've learned and experienced is simply through the act of journaling. What matters is that you have a solid record that you can refer back to throughout your journey.

Other ways of recording what you've learned and experienced are creating pieces of art, video, or composing music.

7.   Integrate and embody your spirituality

It takes much more strength of character, sincerity, and courage to integrate and embody what you've learned actively than to jump into whatever is new and exciting.

This is an organic process that takes time. You cannot rush or force spiritual integration. There are numerous ways to begin the integration and embodiment part of your journey. Some of these inner work and soul work practices include: Meditation, Mindfulness, Contemplations, Breath work, Shadow Work, Self-love, Inner child Work, and Self-inquiry.

Anything that helps you to slow down, be introspective, and go inward while encouraging present-moment awareness will help you to integrate and embody what you experience.

Instead of being a magical-sounding idea, you will actively *live* and express qualities such as loving kindness, presence, and wisdom. But first, you need to be sincere and dedicated to this path.

I wish you well on your path. Remember it's not a destination, but a journey.

Don't forget to recommend
The Gumbeaux Sistahs series
for your next book club meeting!

Reading group guide available at
www.gumbeauxsistahs.com

HOW TO START YOUR OWN GUMBEAUX SISTAHS GROUP

The Gumbeaux Sistahs books are all about women supporting women and getting the most out of life at the same time.

Women need other women to hash over and discuss our unique challenges and joys of our lives. It's healthy to share our feelings, learn from one another, and realize we are not alone. And let's face it—it's a lot of fun.

So let's do it! Here's how:

1.   Make a list of 5-10 women friends or acquaintances. Don't limit yourself at all. This could be a great opportunity to meet with new people you'd like to get to know. Food, drinks, and fun are your best draw. Decide on a theme you'd like to suggest—it could be that every meeting has a new topic to discuss, i.e. the challenges of ageing, the changing roles of women in the home, children/grandchildren challenges,

do you feel invisible? DIY projects. Books to recommend. Dining out. There are so many topics, and you could take turns coming up with the next meeting's topic. Invite the women on your list to an initial meeting with this invite or one like it:

> *You are invited! Women need women to discuss our passages of life with its many hills and valleys. We all have a need to share our feelings, learn from one another, and realize we are not alone. Please join me at my home (or wherever) monthly and become part of the conversation. I value you, your opinions, and your manner of interacting with others. Please join my group.*

Add the details of time, place, and if it's to be a potluck, etc. And that's that!

2. At the initial meeting—discuss why you wanted to form the group. Decide on where, when and how often to meet.

3. Choose a coordinator just to help keep things organized. An assistant isn't a bad idea either.

4. If you have time at the initial meeting, introduce a topic to give everyone an idea of how the meetings will go in the future.

5. Decide what the topic will be for the next month. Here are some suggestions:

- Beauty and appearance
- Business/Work
- Charity
- Entertainment
- Exercise
- Family

- Fashion
- Field Trips
- Finance
- Friendship
- Gardening
- Goals
- Happiness
- Health
- How to have happy Home Life
- Laughter
- Learning
- Legal Issues
- Mental acuity
- Marriage
- Motherhood
- Outside Speakers or Services
- Parenting
- Peacefulness
- People Focus
- Personalities
- Roles in society
- Romance
- Self-Awareness
- Self-Help
- Spirituality
- Yoga

6. Send out reminders when it gets close to your next meeting date.

7. Please email Jax, and let her know how it's going—she wants in on the good times! www.gumbeauxsistahs.com

8. Your group may eventually expand from this initial format. Some groups lunch together, share book club notes together, volunteer for good causes, and even travel together.

9. Finally, and most importantly—don't forget to have a ridiculous amount of fun!

ACKNOWLEDGMENTS

What in the world would I do without my readers? I want to say thank you to you all for your readership, your encouragement, and your gumbeaux-ship! It is pure joy for me to write these books with you in mind. So thank you, thank you, thank you!

I also want to thank Elizabeth Frey, my unrelenting (read "pushy") and adored editor for sussing out plot holes, and my penchant for waaaay too many commas,,,,,!

And many thanks go to my Gumbeaux Sistahs groups (including my own) for adding joy and laughter to my life as well as their own. Gumbeaux rules!

And finally, to my friend and Astrology/Tarot Reader, Sondraya, who, as of this printing, is still offering her services by phone and in person in Sedona, Arizona. Love to you, sistah!

Life is short—eat the gumbeaux, sistahs!

Love,
Jax

ABOUT THE AUTHOR

orn in New Orleans, Jax Frey came into this world with a sense of celebration of culture, food, family, and fun. Translating that celebration into her writing and onto canvas is her true calling. Her colorful art depicts everything from her dancing *Gumbeaux Sistahs* paintings to her popular line of original Mini paintings. Over 30,000 original mini paintings have been created and sold into art collections worldwide, and Jax holds a World Record for *The Most Original Acrylic Paintings on Canvas by One Artist.*

Jax Frey

Jax splits her time between New Orleans and Natchez, MS and can be found writing in her favorite local coffeehouses everyday with her loveable, incorrigible pug/tornadoes, Lucy and Ethel.

Contact Jax for her available dates for book signings, zoom meetings, and speaking engagements. www.gumbeauxsistahs.com

And Sign up for the *Gumbeaux Sistahs* newsletter at www.gumbeauxsistahs.com

FB and Instagram: **Gumbeaux Sistahs**
Jax's art can be seen at: www.artbyjax.com
Facebook and Instagram: **Jax Frey**

WE LOVE REVIEWS!

Dear Readers:

Reviews on **Amazon.com and social media** are the biggest compliment you can pay a writer. Please share your reading experience of *The Gumbeaux Sistahs* novels:

— Help others make good book choices
— Help your authors get the word out about their work.

<u>So, if you enjoyed the book,</u> please leave a review of your favorite Gumbeaux Sistahs novel on www.amazon.com and share on Social Media. Thanks for the Gumbeaux love!

Recent Amazon reviews of the Gumbeaux Sistahs:

"I loved this book. I can so relate to it. People in Louisiana are like this! I can't wait to share this book with my own sistahs!"

"I absolutely LOVED this book, the style, and description of characters. I went on a cruise and read this book in 1 day! I couldn't put it down. GREAT book, especially if you know the area it takes place in. It's about community, helping one another out and just doing life together. A MUST read in your collection! Oprah needs to endorse it!! Just saying!"

"This is a great read for immersing yourself in the fun-loving, warmhearted, feel-good camaraderie that abounds in small Southern towns. The characters are quirky and interesting and find solutions to life's challenges over gumbo and wine. Just like my friends and me!"

OTHER BOOKS BY JAX FREY

<u>*The Gumbeaux Sistahs*</u>
(1st book in *Gumbeaux Sistahs* series)

Five fiery, Southern women wage a hilarious war against the problems of a sistah-in-trouble, using their improbable friendships, unpredictable schemes, oh-so-numerous cocktails, and a shared passion for good gumbo. *The Gumbeaux Sistahs* is a heartwarming, laugh-out-loud story you won't want to put down.

The Gumbeaux Sistahs is an official selection of the Pulpwood Queens
(The largest book club in the world with
over 800 book clubs registered)

Gumbeaux Love

(2nd book in the *Gumbeaux Sistahs* series)

Single, Southern artist Judith Lafferty casually confesses to her Gumbeaux Sistahs that she is occasionally lonely and would like to fall in love again. Seriously—you'd think that by now she would know to keep her mouth shut around these women. The Sistahs tackle her problem, along with their own love challenges, with their usual unreasonable, extreme plots and schemes, including a kidnapping, a cupid costume, and trying out pick-up lines at the deli cheese counter. In helping out their friend, the Sistahs help each other as well and bring to light the many flavors of love. Be ready for twists, turns, laugh-out-loud times, and heart-wrenching moments. You'll be sure to recognize yourself and your close friends in the unstoppable sistahs.

Gumbeaux Magic
(3rd Book of the *Gumbeaux Sistahs* series)

Oh my gravy! What's next? You never know when life's magic spells will hit you upside the head, and the Sistahs' tribulations are just getting started. One sistah is arrested, one is widowed, another is threatened by a younger woman, and yet another is dealing with an attempted abduction! If there is one thing this group of unstoppable women is good at, it's getting together for some amazing gumbo and brainstorming the most unexpected solutions to life's difficulties.

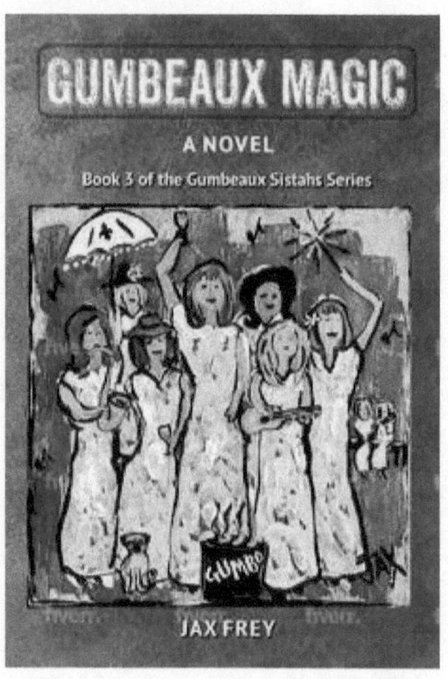

Tales of the Friendship Bench

(4th Book of the *Gumbeaux Sistahs* series)

The Gumbeaux Sistahs all thought it was such a great idea to build a Friendship Bench in front of their art gallery. It was close by, and it offered a safe place and a friendly ear to visitors to talk about their lives and troubles with one sistah or another. The problem was, you never knew who was going to show up! When a thief, a pushy matriarch, a struggling artist, and a stubborn patient visit the bench, the Sistahs are overwhelmed and go scrambling for help. But never underestimate the power of strong friendship—or of a Gumbeaux Sistah!

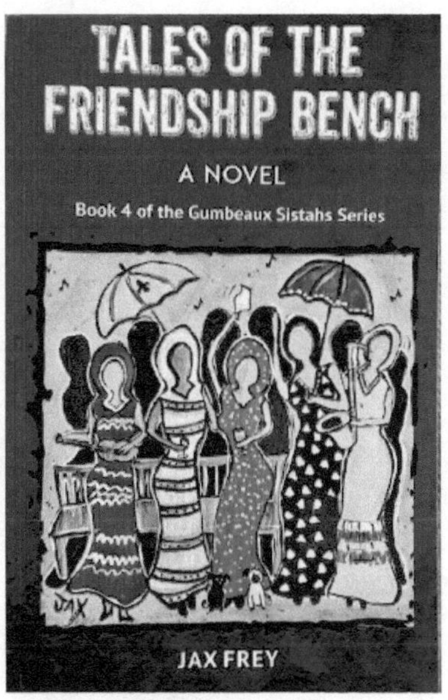

All *Gumbeaux Sistahs* novels are available at **Amazon.com**
in paperback and kindle versions.
Order signed copies of books at www.gumbeauxsistahs.com

Coming Soon

**More adventures with the
Gumbeaux Sistahs!**

**Sign up for the author newsletter to be the first to know when
their next adventure is out at: www.gumbeauxsistahs.com**

READERS' GUIDE
CROW MUSIC
BY JAX FREY

1.   Talk about the spiritual journey in your life. Why is it important to you?

2.   What three words would you use to best describe this book?

3.   What was your favorite moment in the book? Your least favorite?

4.   If you were in charge of casting the movie version of this book, who would you cast as each character?

5.   If you could invite one character over to your house for dinner, who would it be & why?

6. *If you had to trade places with any character in the book, who would you choose & why?*

7. *What surprised you the most when you were reading this book?*

8. *How did the setting of the book impact the story?*

9. *If you had to choose one lesson that the author was trying to teach us with this story, what would it be?*

10. *If you could write one more chapter after the ending, what would you write?*